A LADY IN LOVE

"No one is perfect, Lord Winter," Vivian said softly.

He laughed. "I am so very far from perfect, and so many people would testify to that fact, that I don't know why I ever have a thought about perfection."

Vivian was not pleased by his levity and his quick dismissal of his own worth. "You treat yourself too lightly, my lord. You must remember the worthy things you have done."

"And what would that be?" he asked in amusement.

"You have helped me and my family," she returned, "and, if I asked you, I am quite certain that you would help others."

"Perhaps," he said, "but only if you asked me. I do not go looking for charitable endeavors. In the meantime, it is enough for me to have helped you and given you an opportunity to make a life for yourself. You have given me pleasure, my dear, and I should like to return the favor."

A minute or two later the dance had ended and he had led her into the shadowy garden. "Do you remember our first stroll in a garden?" he asked teasingly.

Vivian smiled. "Of course, Lord Winter. I believe we should be looking for Tom and Mr. Wilding now."

He chuckled. "I wouldn't put it past them." Stopping suddenly, Lord Winter pulled Vivian close to him, until she was aware of every fiber of material in his jacket—and even more aware of how natural it felt to be held in his arms. She did not even murmur when he sank down upon a stone bench in a tiny arbor, gathering her onto his lap and pressing kisses on her neck and shoulders until she could scarcely catch her breath . . .

Books by Mona Gedney

A LADY OF FORTUNE
THE EASTER CHARADE
A VALENTINE'S DAY GAMBIT
A CHRISTMAS BETROTHAL
A SCANDALOUS CHARADE
A DANGEROUS AFFAIR
A LADY OF QUALITY

Published by Zebra Books

A LADY
OF QUALITY

Mona Gedney

Zebra Books
Kensington Publishing Corp.

http://www.zebrabooks.com

ZEBRA BOOKS are published by

Kensington Publishing Corp.
850 Third Avenue
New York, NY 10022

Zebra and the Z logo Reg. U.S. Pat. & TM Off.

First Printing: December, 1996
10 9 8 7 6 5 4 3 2 1

Printed in the United States of America

Chapter One

"I won't do it, Mama! I *can't!*" Vivian stared out the window, her back to her mother. Outside, fog blanketed the garden that rolled down to the steep banks of the cleave where a rocky stream plunged down to the sea. If the fates were kind, she thought, plucking impatiently at the heavy drapery, she would be safely enfolded in that concealing mist, far beyond the sound of her mother's voice.

"But of course you can, my dear," responded Mrs. Reddington faintly, plucking nervously at her embroidery and staring at Vivian's uncompromisingly straight back. The very picture of fluttering indecision herself, she often reflected that having one daughter was proving far more difficult than raising two sons had been. Forcing Vivian to do something that she did not wish to do ranked at the bottom of her list of favored activities.

"But all young ladies of quality are expected to have their coming out, Vivian dear," she added soothingly. "And it won't be difficult at all. In fact, you may well find that you enjoy it.''

Her tone sounded unconvincing, even to herself, and Vivian made a most unladylike noise in response to it. The normal young lady might find the pleasures of a London season enticing, but Vivian was not, of course, the normal young lady. The conversation was proving quite as disagreeable as she had feared it would be. Mrs. Reddington had always thought poorly of women who gave way to spasms to get their own way, but sometimes dealing with her daughter brought to mind the advantages of falling into hysterics.

Vivian shook her head abruptly and smacked a small fist against her open palm, her dark hair tumbling down from its combs as it always did. ''I would rather that you cut me to ribbons or threw me to the sharks! I could bear either of those with fortitude—but *London?* How *could* you force me to go to London, Mama?'' Her tone clearly equated London with the horrors of the rack.

Vivian's intensity had always troubled her mother, but she had comforted herself that the child would grow out of it, particularly once Vivian's older brother Drake was no longer at home to encourage her in her odd, hoydenish ways.

''I can't imagine where you get such ridiculous notions, Vivian!'' Mrs. Reddington replied crossly, giving up her embroidery—and the notion of spasms—entirely. Being of a literal turn of mind herself, she was always inclined to take Vivian's pronouncements at face value. ''You make me sound like the most unnatural parent. The very idea that I could do such a thing to one of my own children!'' The more she thought of it, the more resentful she grew. ''After all, I am only thinking of your own welfare.''

''How can it be for my own welfare?'' demanded Vivian, clearly ungrateful for her mother's efforts on her behalf. ''How can it possibly be to my benefit to do something that is so completely foreign to my nature?''

Mrs. Reddington surveyed her offspring gloomily. Vivian's small, piquant face, pale now with an intensity that her dark eyes, always over-large, emphasized unduly, seemed the face and expression of a changeling. She bore not the smallest resemblance to her brothers, her father, her mother—all of whom were reckoned remarkably handsome. Indeed, her only claim to beauty was her eyes and her thick mane of shining dark hair. She certainly did not possess the face or the bearing of a young lady who could take London by storm.

''The last thing I shall do, Mama,'' Vivian continued relentlessly, ''is to put on airs and simper at a gentleman simply because he *is* a gentleman! And I won't be confined to a stuffy drawing room when I had rather be in the library or out riding on Pimm!''

She paused to take a breath and turned toward her mother, her exasperation increasing when she saw that they were no longer alone. A very pretty young woman, wearing what Vivian and Drake had always called her cat-in-the-creampot expression, had seated herself demurely next to Mrs. Reddington and was patting that lady's hand sympathetically. Vivian's dark brows grew closer together and she continued fiercely.

''You know very well, Mama, that I would rather have my eyebrows plucked with red-hot pincers than to be like Lacey and try to think of some emptyheaded thing to say to gentlemen that I care nothing about! I simply shall *not* do it, Mama—no matter what you and John want! If Drake were here, he wouldn't allow you to do this to me!''

She walked to the door of the drawing room, paused a moment for dramatic effect—as though being led to the scaffold—then made her exit.

Her long-suffering mother, with a wisdom born of painful experience, made no attempt to stop her or to argue with her further, but turned to Vivian's cousin Lacey with raised eyebrows and a sigh.

"I *told* John that she would fly up into the boughs at the first mention of taking her to London for the season. And I knew that I wouldn't be able to make her see reason—at least not the first time we spoke of it."

She did not mention that she had prevented John from being the one to break the news to his sister; Vivian's distaste for him would have instantly sounded the death knell for their plans. "You may be the head of the household," she had told him, "but I am still your mother and *I* will speak to my daughter about her coming out." Nor did she add that John had told her privately that he saw little prospect of Vivian's receiving an eligible offer.

"You did your best, Aunt," said the young lady soothingly. "You mustn't mind what Vivian says. In time she will come to see that you are quite right."

"You are such a comfort to me, Lacey," replied Mrs. Reddington absently—and with only partial sincerity. "I only wish that I could believe that Vivian *will* change her mind—because as a rule, you know, she doesn't. Drake wrote from the Peninsula that as yet he hadn't met any mule that could match her for stubbornness. It was most ungentlemanly of him to say so, of course—not that it upset Vivian, for she laughed about it—but it was quite an accurate description, nonetheless."

Lacey set her lips primly at the mention of Drake. "I'm sure that I should hate to hear any gentleman—even my own brother, if I had one—express such an opinion of me."

"And no one would, my dear," Mrs. Reddington assured her. "You and Vivian are as different as chalk and cheese."

Nothing could have been truer. Eustacia Lavenham, the only child of Mrs. Reddington's late sister, had lived with them at Trevelyan since her mother's death years ago, and she was everything that Vivian was not—demure, dainty, flutteringly feminine. It was a contrast that Eustacia had always employed to her advantage, drawing attention in the kindest manner to dear Vivian's shortcomings.

"And to say such things to my own dear mama—if she were still here—why, I simply cannot imagine myself doing such a thing," continued that young lady somewhat tactlessly. "You must feel it terribly, Aunt. Vivian must certainly learn to guard her tongue. No gentleman likes to hear a young lady speak in such a fashion."

Mrs. Reddington, although in complete agreement with her niece, found herself defending her rebellious offspring. Eustacia often had that effect upon people.

"Of course, she hasn't your placid disposition, Lacey dear," Mrs. Reddington demurred. "She feels things very intensely, you know. Why, she moped about for days when one of Drake's hunting dogs was caught in that trap some poacher had set over in the woods along the cleave."

"All that fuss over a mere animal," sniffed Eustacia unsympathetically. "I will always believe that she simply wanted more attention from you and Drake—and you gave it to her, of course. Vivian really is unspeakably spoiled, Aunt. I don't know how you will be able to persuade her to go to London when she doesn't wish to do so."

Even though she resented her niece's comments, Mrs. Reddington had reached much the same conclusion herself. "I know, Lacey," she sighed. "When Vivian takes it into her head not to do something, she simply will not budge."

They sat silently for a moment, each of them lost in her own thoughts. Eustacia was inclined to hope that she would still have a season of her own in London, without the inconvenience of the wayward Vivian, but it did not seem likely that Mrs. Reddington could be persuaded to leave Vivian to her own devices while she jaunted off to London with her niece.

Mrs. Reddington, on the other hand, had not quite despaired

of convincing her daughter that it was in the interest of her own happiness to go to London for the Season. John had made up his mind that he would marry soon—when he found a young woman worthy of him, of course—and then Mrs. Reddington and Vivian would become guests in their own home, with the new Mrs. John Reddington presiding over Trevelyan. Mrs. Reddington could accept that; her disposition was pliable and she would be able to suit her ways to those of John and his future wife.

For Vivian, however, things were quite otherwise. After all, she would certainly not wish to live out her life under the care of John, with whom she got on very poorly, and she would certainly not wish to see him and his wife officially in charge of Trevelyan. Nor did her beloved Drake, now gallivanting across the Peninsula in the pay of Wellington, show any signs of settling down and establishing a household of his own where she might make her residence as a maiden aunt. The conclusion was inescapable: the only happy solution for Vivian was to make a satisfactory marriage.

Mrs. Reddington had not allowed herself to define what a "satisfactory marriage" for her wayward daughter might be. Instead, she had entertained vague visions of some agreeable young man who would provide her daughter with horses and children in some country place. If Vivian could only be persuaded to see London as a means to a happier end, she might view the whole matter of her coming out in a different light.

She had not yet shared with Vivian the news that John intended to take a bride. Knowing how the prospect of such a change in their circumstances would distress her daughter, Mrs. Reddington was determined to play that as her final card only if Vivian continued flatly to refuse to go to London. It would be infinitely better if she could meet someone, become happily engaged, and then learn that John would be bringing a bride home to Trevelyan.

Mrs. Reddington had written to Drake about the problem several weeks ago, and had hopes of hearing from him soon. Vivian would listen to him when she would hear no one else in the world.

Even if she agreed to go, however, Mrs. Reddington knew that a successful outcome was far from guaranteed. John's unwelcome words still rang in her ears. "She has no fortune and is too plain and too headstrong to take—in London or any other place," he had said dryly. "Since she cannot be persuaded to hold her tongue and listen to her betters, I cannot imagine any man of sense making an offer for her. I fear that I shall have her on my hands forever."

How very like John that was, Mrs. Reddington reflected bitterly, to say the unthinkable and act as though he had done all that was proper. Even though it was his duty as the elder son to take care of Vivian, he felt no real obligation to do so and had once again removed to the snug little property in Scotland that he had inherited from a great uncle, sending an occasional message to them back in England. Trevelyan, he said, had little to commend itself, being too far from good company and offering little in the way of good hunting and fishing. His home in Scotland, on the other hand, offered everything he could wish and it was the place where he chose to spend most of his time.

"Leaving me to take care of everything here at Trevelyan while he fishes and hunts!" his mother had fumed in a letter to Drake. "He is the image of his father—occupied by his own interests and caring nothing for anyone else—not even his own family! It was well enough when he had no one to consider but himself, but when your father died, he became the head of the family, and it is more than time that he behaved as though he were! You are making your own way in the world, and John doesn't wish to settle even a farthing on Vivian. Your father always saw fit to leave me down in this godforsaken country house, saying that it was a healthy place to rear his children, when what he meant was that it was inconvenient to have us in town with him! John is his image—and I will *not* have it!" She had underscored "not" several times to emphasize the strength of her conviction.

Mrs. Reddington was never a particularly steady person at the best of times, but now, deprived as she was of the company of both of her sons and living in the comparative isolation of Trevelyan, Vivian's careless manners had weighed more and more heavily upon her. Fearful that the girl would do something so outrageous as to make herself a social pariah, Mrs. Reddington had determined that she would have her coming out in the spring, despite the fact that she would scarcely have turned seventeen.

"Better to have her settled early than to have her do something that will set the ton in a bustle and put her beyond the pale," she had remarked wisely to Drake in her letter.

"If only dear Drake will write and tell her she must go to London, all will be well," said Mrs. Reddington to Eustacia. "I must trust that we will hear from him soon."

"Oh, yes, dear *dear* Drake," sighed her niece. "Surely we will hear soon, Aunt. I wrote a note to him, too," she added coyly. "I only hope that he will spare the time to remember me with a letter."

Mrs. Reddington, recalling the fact that she had received only two letters herself from Drake during his past months abroad, responded somewhat tartly. "I would be happy merely to know that my dear boy is well and out of harm's way." Eustacia's interest in Drake had not escaped her attention, and she was not particularly pleased by it. It was quite as necessary for him to marry well as it was for Vivian. "If he has an opportunity to send any letter at all, it will surely be to Vivian. They are extraordinarily fond of one another, and Drake knows how important to Vivian I consider this season in London."

Eustacia's lovely lips thinned. "Yes, I have had their fondness for one another pointed out to me. Although it pains me to say it, I fear it is partially Drake's fault that Vivian is so headstrong. He has done nothing but encourage her in her headlong ways."

Noting the displeasure on her aunt's face, she added smoothly, "And as I said before, Aunt, Vivian is far too heedless in her treatment of you. She should be grateful to you for your kindness." Here she smiled self-consciously and added with a pretty hesitancy, "*I* am most grateful to you, Aunt, for your generous offer to give me a coming out as well. I shall do my best to make you proud of me."

Although Vivian's behavior had always been beyond her comprehension, Lacey at least could be depended upon to act in a manner befitting a lady, reflected Mrs. Reddington somewhat grudgingly. There was nothing singular about her behavior. Lovely though she undoubtedly was, she was not an exciting child, but Drake and Vivian had always supplied more than enough excitement for the household. And, although Lacey could occasionally be irritating, she did, on the whole, mean well.

Vivian regarded her in a less favorable light, however. From the time Lacey had come to them at the age of eleven, she had been a priggish carrier of tales, and over and over again she had been responsible for exposing Vivian's peccadilloes while preening herself upon the differences between them. Drake had not been taken in by her tactics, but the much older John and—to an extent—Mrs. Reddington considered Lacey a model of good behavior and never missed an opportunity to point out her many virtues to the careless Vivian.

Reared at Trevelyan, an isolated estate on the cliffs overlooking the Bristol Channel, Vivian had divided her childhood between reading and writing bloodcurdling tales in her father's library and running wild in the countryside, riding her pony fearlessly into the loneliest stretches of woods and climbing down the steep cliffs to look for smugglers' caves along the shore. Her friends were not always those her mother would have chosen for her—many, in fact, she knew nothing about. Happily, she had been able to keep most of them a secret from Lacey, too. Even Tom Cane, her childhood partner in mischief, was unaware of them, for, being three years her elder and a boy to boot, he had gone away to school before she had met most of them. When he returned for occasional brief visits, he was no longer her Tom, but a young gentleman who disapproved of her wild ways and exerted himself to be a good influence upon her, so she had felt no need to share her new friends with him.

Vivian was not particularly cautious by nature, but even she recognized that Mrs. Reddington might be justified in her objections to old Ben Marley, keeper of The Lighthouse, a small, down-at-the-heels hostelry set on a lonely headland overlooking the Channel. Although it was frequented by some of the hardier locals, The Lighthouse had the reputation of being a smugglers' inn. It was, in fact, a reputation that was fully justified.

She wisely kept her visits there to herself, a secret even from her beloved Drake, but old Ben had been her friend since she was ten, when he had found her scrabbling about in one of the caves used by some of his "gentlemen" just as the tide was coming in. He had whisked her out before she could examine the contents so recently deposited in its recesses—also before the tide could trap her there, for the thin strip of rocky beach was rapidly disappearing. She had been wet and cold and he had taken her to The Lighthouse for a warm drink—and they had been fast friends ever since.

It was to The Lighthouse that she turned Pimm now, eager to put behind her the troubles of the afternoon. A friendly chat with Ben, or just the chance to sit on the cliffs and watch their colors shifting in the changing light of the afternoon sun and to listen to the water pounding against the rocks below, would be enough to make her feel that all was well again.

It did not trouble her that her behavior was not that of the conventional young lady. From the time she was four, when she had slipped away from her elderly nurse to follow a group of passing gypsies, she had chafed at the restrictions placed upon a young female of quality. She had been greatly incensed when their leader, a handsome young man with a flashing smile and no desire to be accused of kidnapping one of the local gentry, returned her to her frantic nurse.

Independent and careless of the opinion of others, she had always led her family a merry chase, and even now that she had reached a marriageable age she was showing no sign of changing her ways. The much older John, the head of the family since her father's death, regarded her with ill-concealed irritation, her madcap brother Drake—much closer to her in years and in temperament—with amusement, and her mother with a deep-seated anxiety. Vivian did not care for the role she had been dealt by fate and society, nor did she have the slightest intention of playing it.

Seated now on Pimm, her surefooted pony, she brooded over her dilemma as he picked his way carefully along the rocky cliff path high above the Channel. She had hoped that her mother would not attempt to press her on the subject of marriage—certainly she had made her feelings on the subject perfectly clear time and time again. The only men worth marrying existed only in the pages of a book. So far as she had been able to discern, there was no connection between the vigorous, exciting personalities in the stories she read and those that were to be encountered in the real life of a "lady of quality." So far as she could see, it would be better to marry even a rakehell from one of the novels and to live a life of sorrow and pain than to marry some dull modern gentleman who would bore her into an early grave. However, since she had no desire to do either, she was quite determined to live her life in her own way, free to make her own decisions. How to manage it in the face of her family's interference was the problem.

Sighing, she reined in her pony and stared off in the direction of the Channel. Had there been no fog, she could have watched the ships making their way to Bristol and back again and dreamed of running away to sea as she had wished to do as a child. On the far side of the Channel, too, lay the soft hills of the Welsh shore, waiting to be explored. No vexation offered by John or Lacey had ever been able to hold its own against the pleasure of such daydreams or against the exhilaration of a wild gallop across the moors on Pimm.

Denied both of these consolations by the fog, Vivian decided to seek comfort at The Lighthouse. Ben had been after her to give up coming there, reminding her that she was no longer a child, but she had countered by saying there was no harm in it so long as no one knew. She never had to worry about being seen as she entered—and thus reported to her mother—for, like all good smugglers' inns, it had its share of secret entrances. Today's heavy fog made her doubly safe.

Silently turning her pony off the cliff-top path and into the sheltering shadows of the woods, she followed a narrow trail, pausing a moment to listen before cautiously slipping from the saddle. Holding back part of a bush that concealed an even narrower pathway, she waited while Pimm moved by her with the assurance of one who had done this many times before, then let the branches slip gently back into place. Another twenty feet brought them to their destination.

Tethering Pimm securely in the shadows of a cave, she stepped farther into the darkness and pushed aside a rock that concealed the handle of a low door. Easing it open, she ducked quickly in and shut it behind her. The old inn, used by smugglers for decades, perched high atop the cliff, the land dropping abruptly away behind it, and the wine cellar had hidden beneath it yet another cellar whose entrance and exit remained a secret from the excisemen who, upon very rare occasions, chose to investigate The Lighthouse.

It was into this hidden cellar that Vivian stepped. Darkness surrounded her immediately, but she was untroubled. With the ease born of familiarity, Vivian reached through the blackness and took a candlestick from the shelf to the right of the entrance. Below it were several kegs of brandy. Lighting the candle carefully, she extracted a bundle from one of the kegs. After slipping out of her riding habit, she pulled on the rough garb of a fisherman and tucked her hair up under her cap. The disguise had worked well enough in the past for her to be able to sit unnoticed in the chimney corner and listen to the men in the taproom without drawing attention to herself. Indeed, her presence was taken for granted, having long ago been pointed out as "Ben's nevvy, Bobby," a quiet lad who helped his uncle in "the trade." She had even helped—under cover of darkness, of course—to unload some of the shipments into Ben's caves at the base of the inn.

As she had expected, the taproom was crowded, most of the customers being sailors or fishermen who had been kept from their trade by the gathering fog and the threat of rough weather. Gratefully she sank into her chimney corner, glad of the fire against the damp chill of the afternoon, and listened comfortably to the rough voices of the men.

"Aye, the cutter's still out there," muttered a wide-shouldered seaman in a rough blue jacket, seated at a table close by. "We sowed the crop, howsoever, so we be safe enough."

"For the time being," replied his companion dryly. "I fear that tonight may be another story."

At the sound of such a cultivated voice, very out of place in this group, Vivian sat up abruptly and tried to see the speaker through the gathering gloom of the long, narrow room, which was lighted only by the fire and two tiny windows. She could discern simply a tall figure wrapped in a dark coat, but she smiled. It must be Lord Lucifer—or so she had named him in the story she was writing. Who he actually was, she had no idea, for Ben was very circumspect about his dealings in the trade. That he was a member of the nobility—as well as a smuggler—she had no doubt. He was clearly as proud as Lucifer, an observation which had originally given her the inspiration for his name, and he was as elegantly tall and dark and dangerous-looking as his namesake was reputed to be. She had heard one of the smugglers whispering to another about the man, saying that he had killed his own brother for his title and fortune. Vivian had immediately incorporated that into her story. She had been torn between making him the hero of her tale and making him the villain. As yet she had not decided which it was to be.

"Put your mind at ease, sir," returned the man in the blue jacket confidently. "No gauger is going to have his hooks into this crop. It'll be safe delivered this very night."

"See that it is. I've no wish to lose this lot." Lord Lucifer's tone was short, and Vivian could see that he placed little confidence in the speaker. She also saw that he passed the man in the blue jacket a folded square of paper, and nothing but a brief glance passed between them as the seaman slipped it quickly into an inside pocket.

Here Lord Lucifer turned toward the fire and Vivian had her first clear view of his face. His was a striking countenance, its dramatic effect heightened by a long, narrow scar on his left cheek. Vivian drank it all in, congratulating herself silently on her great good luck in seeing him at close range at last. Now she would be able to describe her character precisely.

It must surely be a scar from a duel, she decided, studying it carefully through her lowered lashes. Nothing could be better for her story. Immediately she began to conjure up the various explanations possible for the scar. That he had killed his man, she was certain. But had he been defending the honor of his sister or his wife? Or had his motive been more mysterious, less honorable? Cupping her chin in both hands, she let her imagination roam at will, forgetting where she was.

Lost in thought as she was, Vivian was not aware that her subject had come closer to the fire.

"Are you a sailor, boy?" The question was abrupt and the voice unmistakable. Vivian jumped, her heart racing uncomfortably.

"This is my sister's boy, your lordship," said Ben, moving deftly between them and giving Vivian's shoulders a little shake. "Mind your manners, Bobby."

Duly reminded of her position, Vivian bobbed her head and moved as though to pull on an imaginary forelock, keeping her head well down.

"Helps me here and there, Bobby does," Ben continued comfortably, "but, as you can see, he's not much of a gabster."

"So I see." Lord Lucifer sounded mildly amused, but Vivian kept her eyes carefully lowered. "That is not such a bad thing, however. Perhaps he will be of some assistance to me tonight."

"My sister has been poorly, but if she can spare him, he'll be with us." Vivian could feel Ben's hand firmly upon her shoulder and she knew that it boded no good for her. He had warned her that she had to give up coming to The Lighthouse, particularly when there were people about.

"Suit yourself, Marley," replied Lucifer, his voice indicating that he had already lost interest in the subject. "Just be certain that the job gets done. I shall be watching tonight."

Ben's hand remained clamped upon her shoulder, and Vivian could see only his lordship's high leather boots and the hem of his many-caped greatcoat as he turned to go. The same hand guided her firmly back the way she had come, seeing her all the way down to the second cellar.

"You have to give over coming here, Miss," Ben told her firmly, his brown eyes serious below thatched gray eyebrows. "You've grown too old to play such tricks."

"Nonsense, Ben," Vivian replied lightly. "No one thinks anything of me. After all, aren't I your 'nevvy, Bobby'? Wouldn't they wonder what had happened to me if I suddenly stopped coming?"

He shook his head. "Not if I was to tell them you've taken ship with a merchantman."

Vivian looked at him in exasperation. "And then I suppose after a decent interval you'll tell them that I died at sea!"

Ben nodded briskly. "But I'll give you a brave death, never fear, Miss," he said reassuringly. "Nothing cowhearted."

"But I don't want to stop coming, Ben! Why, I've been spending time here for seven years. Why must I suddenly stop now?"

"Because, Miss," he responded patiently, "you be too old to play the part of a lad. Soon or late you'll be caught out at it, and then there'll be the devil to pay for both of us."

He stared at her a moment and his bushy gray eyebrows grew closer together. "You hear what I am saying now, Miss Vivian, for I mean it. I know that you would not be wishing to get me in real trouble."

Vivian didn't reply, recognizing with a sinking heart the earnestness in his voice. Ben meant what he was saying. He wasn't going to let her return.

She brooded over this unpleasant turn of events during her quiet ride home, and, as the gathering storm began to break, she made up her mind. Ben or no Ben, she would go one last time to help them harvest the crop. After all, Lord Lucifer would be there tonight and she needed to study him for her book—and she deserved one farewell visit to The Lighthouse.

Chapter Two

Leaving her home secretly that night presented no great challenge for Vivian. She had done it often enough in the years past, having been ably schooled in the art of escape by Drake. When her mother and Lacey had retired for the evening, she waited patiently for more than half an hour, then, dressed in some of Drake's old gear—dark trousers, leather boots and a dark, rough woolen smock over all—she tucked her hair under a cap. Quite as though it had a mind of its own, however, it worked its way from under the cap almost immediately. Since she could not risk having that happen again, Vivian went to her dressing table, drew out a pair of shears, and ruthlessly hacked off her hair just below the ears. Then she put the cap on again, noting with satisfaction that it stayed in place nicely, and crept downstairs. The rain had stopped for the moment, but the gusting wind effectively covered the noise of any creaking floorboards.

Quietly she let herself out a side door and hurried toward the stable. She saddled Pimm in a very few minutes, and they were soon on their way—not to The Lighthouse, but to the beach that ran along the base of the cliff below the inn. The seaman in the blue jacket had said that they had sown the crop, so she knew that the tubs of brandy had been dropped overboard, their position marked for a later harvesting. Many of the tubs would be delivered to waiting customers immediately, while some would have to be stored beyond the prying eyes of the preventive waterguard.

Tonight's stormy sea offered an opportune moment to pick them up, for it assured the free traders that they would not be set upon by any wandering excisemen. Although the forces of the law had not been particularly active along their part of the coast for some time, knowing an impossible job when they saw it, Ben was always careful. Most of the people living along the coast regarded free trading as a legitimate business and were inclined to view the officers of the law as interfering busybodies, but occasionally someone was arrested, and there was talk of a new officer at Lynhurst who would like to make a name for himself by ridding the area of smugglers.

Vivian, who learned all the gossip of the neighborhood from Joe in the stables and Betsy, a kitchenmaid from the village whom she had taught to read, knew that Ben was not the reason the government had sent a new officer to the area. The reason was Hawkins.

James Hawkins had survived a shipwreck two years ago and, being a handsome man and very taking in his ways, according to Betsy, who had seen him several times in the village, he had soon won the heart of Sarah Gibbons, the only child of William Gibbons and the heir to the considerable fortune made in his glassworks. As soon as her father had died, Sarah had married her handsome James, and he had, unfortunately, proved to be very taking in his ways in a more literal sense. In the matter of a few months, he had made her home the headquarters of a gang of smugglers.

"Only they be not honest free traders, Miss," Joe had told her hotly. "They be murderers and thieves, and no honest man would let his wife nor child come next or nigh them. They'll be the ruination of this part of the coast if they keep to their skullduggery."

Vivian had listened wide-eyed to his tales of the evil they had done, and she was grateful that Grassmere, the estate of Sarah Gibbons, was a goodly distance from their own. Hawkins and his men kept themselves busy with a more distant portion of the coast and, according to the stories, they were doing a very brisk trade, although instances of violence were growing more frequent. Ben and his men were of a more peaceful breed, and their activities were very low-key. "Being not wishful of drawing attention to ourselves," Ben had once explained to her.

With this in mind, she was certain that the new riding officer was occupying himself with much bigger fish than Ben, and she felt no anxiety about tonight. Vivian had had the opportunity to help Ben on several such occasions before, but he had discouraged her putting in an appearance, saying that it had grown too dangerous to allow her to come along. She had great faith in Ben's ability to evade any traps, however, and very little fear of the new riding officer, whom she had seen once down in the village. He appeared very young and far too sure of himself, scarcely a match for the experienced and wily members of the brotherhood.

Again she left Pimm tethered securely, this time in the deep shadows of a spinney at the top of the cliff and, after cautiously blacking her face with a little dirt even though there was no bright moonlight, she scrambled down a narrow path toward the little group working on the beach. Working silently and quickly, the men were carrying the tubs, which had been roped in pairs, over their shoulders from the shoreline to a waiting cart.

Vivian was halfway down the path when she heard a shot. Freezing in place, her back against the cliff, she tried to see what was happening below her.

Everything was silent for a moment, except for the pounding of the waves against the sand, and then another shot rang out.

"I am an officer of the law! Stop where you are!" The voice carried clearly above the roar of the surf.

A laugh rang out below. "You'd best be going home to your mother, laddie!" called a voice brightly. It was Ben; Vivian recognized his merry laugh. How many times she had heard the sound, always comforting and happy.

Here another voice was heard, and Vivian strained to catch the words. *"You'd* best go home, old man! Your day is done!" The voice was deep, almost gutteral—and then another shot rang out.

Everything below became chaotic. Try as she would, Vivian could not determine what was taking place. People were running and she heard Ben's name called out once.

Determined not to return home without being certain that all was well with Ben, Vivian continued her way down the narrow path. Once on the beach, she ducked behind the cart, which was partially loaded with the tubs of brandy while the others lay scattered on the sand.

"It's Ben's nevvy!" she heard someone whisper hoarsely, and then a strong hand clapped down upon her shoulder. "You must get your uncle home now, boy!" the voice whispered hoarsely. "He's hurt and he needs your help!"

Vivian, who could now see that the figure slumped against the wheel of the cart was Ben, hurried forward. Blood was flowing quickly from a wound in his shoulder, and even in the dim light afforded by the shifting clouds, she could see the dark stain spreading.

"Unharness that horse!" she whispered fiercely, pointing to the cart and its single horse.

"Nay, lad! How will we take the brandy if we do that?" Here another shot rang out, bouncing off the rocky cliffside above their heads.

"Forget the brandy!" whispered Vivian fiercely, making her voice as low and masculine as she could. "Get out and leave the brandy t' the officer—and t' whoever it be that's with him!"

"The lad's right!" whispered another voice. "Let's take ourselves safe away and leave the brandy!"

Apparently an agreement was reached, and Vivian found herself leading the ancient horse, bearing the unconscious form of Ben Marley, up the narrow, rocky path, hoping that the moon would not suddenly slip from behind the scudding clouds and show their position to those on the beach.

"Oh, Ben!" she murmured to herself as she led the horse carefully along. "What am I to do with you? I can't take you back to The Lighthouse, and I must take care of your wound!"

Once at the top of the cliff, she made her way swiftly to Pimm, and made her decision. Ben must have help. Her mother would die of an attack of apoplexy if she were approached in the middle of the night about helping a smuggler, but Joe would not. Resolutely she made her way home, and quietly rousted Joe from his cot in the room adjoining the stable.

"Can you help him, Joe?" she asked urgently, her voice low as the wide-eyed Joe peered at the wound by candlelight.

"I can try, Miss," he said hesitantly. "But I'm more used to taking care of horses."

"You'll do fine, Joe," Vivian whispered encouragingly. "I don't know anyone who does so well with horses—Ben will be grateful if you can but help him enough so that I can get him back to The Lighthouse."

"You get him back to The Lighthouse?" whispered Joe, scandalized. "You be a lady, Miss! You'll do no such thing! I'll clean the wound and get him safely home!"

Joe was as good as his word. Ben, apparently none the worse for wear, was back at The Lighthouse the next day, waiting on tables as though there were nothing at all amiss. When the riding officer from Lynhurst, young Lieutenant Waring, came to call, Ben served him with a smile, wiping the table clean before him.

"Quite well are you, innkeeper?" asked young Waring, studying his quarry carefully.

"Never better, your lordship," responded Ben heartily.

"You need not address me as 'your lordship,' Marley," said Waring shortly, "as I am certain you know."

"Whatever you say, sir," said Ben cheerily, his bright spirits evidently further oppressing Lieutenant Waring. "Out for a ride today, are you, sir?"

"Yes, Marley—out for a ride, indeed," responded his quarry dismally. "Feeling very well, are you?"

"Never better, sir," said Ben firmly, taking Waring's mug and refilling it at the tap. "And I hope you are feeling the same."

"Yes, yes of course," said Waring more dismally still, staring at his mug of ale. "How could it be otherwise?"

"How indeed, sir?" said Ben heartily. "You must come by more often. The doors of The Lighthouse are always open to you."

Young Waring stared at his host closely, watching for any telltale sign of weakness of injury, then gave it up for lost. "I thank you, innkeeper," he said briskly, trying to act as though everything had gone quite as he had wished. "I shall be back, of course."

"Of course," answered Ben, smiling widely.

When the door closed behind Lieutenant Waring, Ben sank suddenly onto a stool behind the bar and buried his head in his hands.

Vivian, who had been watching from behind a nearby door,

hurried into the empty taproom. "Do you need to lie down, Ben?" she asked, worried by his sudden pallor.

He shook his head. "I'll be all right, Miss," he said in a low voice, "but you must promise me that you'll not come down here again. What if he had seen you?"

"Don't ask me to promise that, Ben!" she pleaded. "You know I'll come again to see how you are getting on."

He shook his head. "It's getting too dangerous, Miss, and so I've told you. Last night it wasn't only Lieutenant Waring that was there, you know. He's such a babe in the woods that I'd not fear him—it was Hawkins!"

To her dismay, Vivian felt her knees grow rubbery. "Hawkins?" she whispered. "What was Hawkins doing on your beach, Ben?"

Ben grimaced. "He's decided that he'll be taking control of everything along this coast, Miss, no matter how small. He was showing me that I'd best be mindful of him."

"He's the one that shot you!" exclaimed Vivian, horrified. "I thought it must have been Lieutenant Waring. At least he would have had a reason to do so!"

Ben shook his head. "Waring shot above us. Hawkins shot to wound—this time. Another time he'll not miss."

"You mean that he would kill you?" demanded Vivian, horrified.

Ben nodded. "He would kill me, you, whoever it would take to make us believe that he means to control the coast."

He stared at her a moment, his dark eyes kindly. "That's why, Miss, you must not be coming here again. He'd kill you or me without a thought—do you understand, Miss?"

Vivian nodded. She understood. If she came to The Lighthouse again, she would be endangering Ben, for he would try to take care of her and would forget about himself. And she couldn't do it.

Rising to leave, she smiled at him. "Thank you, Ben." She

squeezed his hand. "After Drake and Tom went away, I'd have had little happiness without you."

Marley smiled back up at her, relieved that she had understood at last. "And you, Miss. Thank you for last night. And thank the boy that works for you. Without the two of you, I'd never have made it—and I'll not forget it."

Leaning down, Vivian kissed his ruddy cheek soundly. "You've been my faithful friend, Ben—how could I have done any less?"

When Vivian arrived home that evening, her mother had been waiting dinner for quite some time. Fortunately, it was not an unaccustomed matter for her to be late.

"And so, my dear," her mother said as she entered the drawing room, "have you had an interesting day?"

Vivian smiled. "Yes, Mother, indeed I have." Before she could say anything more, Mrs. Reddington looked up from her embroidery and shrieked.

"Your hair, Vivian! Your beautiful hair! Whatever have you done to yourself?"

Vivian shrugged carelessly. "I was tired of having it forever come down round my shoulders, Mama. It was a nuisance."

She looked about the drawing room. Eustacia was watching her with a gently pained expression, quite as though she had expected as much, but was disappointed nonetheless. Since Vivian cared not a fig for what Eustacia expected, she was unmoved.

"I have had a letter from Drake, my dear," said Mrs. Reddington weakly, remembering that she had something of importance to share and forcing herself to look at her daughter and her ragamuffin haircut without flinching. Smiling, she extended the missive to Vivian.

Her color heightened, Vivian snatched it up, smiling at her mother. They were at least agreed upon the happiness of hearing from Drake, and it was comforting to have *something* that they could agree upon, reflected Vivian, unfolding it carefully.

She read it carefully, then studied it once again. She could not be mistaken, even though she wished to be. Drake wished for her to go to London. "Just think of it, my dear," he had written, "if you will but do the pretty in London, we will have more pleasure at home than ever you thought possible. I will give you *Victory* to sail for your own this summer—providing Tom teaches you how to sail her. And as soon as I can come home again, we will take her out together. So think of me and do your best for your dearest Mama and your loving Drake."

She thought rapidly. If Drake wished her to do it, she must of course give the matter serious consideration. And with Ben and The Lighthouse no longer available to her, and Tom occupied with the life of a young gentleman of fashion in London, life here held fewer charms than usual. Then there was the matter of the *Victory*. If Drake gave her the right to use the sailboat, a new avenue to freedom would be opened to her. That, indeed, was the deciding factor. Two months of "doing the pretty" would earn her endless months of pleasure.

Laughing, she held out her arms to her mother. "Do you suppose he truly means that I should entrust my life to Tom, Mama?"

Tom Cane was the son of their nearest neighbor, and during the years of their childhood, he had been prone to disaster. He was the one that twice broke his arm after being thrown from his mount, fell twenty feet from a cliff ledge to the rocky beach below and still bore a twelve-inch scar on his leg to prove it, and had nearly drowned more times than she could count after his father had given him a boat. Although he was now on the town in London, having completed his tour of duty at Oxford, he still regarded Vivian with the barely concealed impatience of an older brother.

Greatly relieved by her response, Mrs. Reddington opened

her arms and enfolded Vivian. "We will do as Drake has bidden us, my dear. I would not have chosen Tom Cane as a teacher for you, but if Drake declares him to be the right choice, then Thomas will indeed teach you how to sail the *Victory*."

"And if I go to London and do all that I am asked, I will be able to have Drake's sailboat?" Vivian demanded, determined to be certain of her prize.

"Indeed you may," her mama assured her, almost limp with relief. "I will see to it myself."

Vivian, thinking of Ben, wounded and scarcely able to make it about his inn, nodded. There would be no more escape for her at The Lighthouse. She would have to find her excitement in another way—and the *Victory* might offer the answer.

"Then I shall do it, Mama," she said. "I shall go to London and I shall force myself to smile and be pleasant."

She paused a moment, then continued. "But I positively will *not* simper, Mama. I shall simply go through the steps of being the docile young lady—I shan't mean a bit of it."

Mrs. Reddington, who would have accepted any terms so long as Vivian agreed to go, smiled and nodded. The first step in her plan had been taken: Vivian was going to London.

Chapter Three

When they arrived in London, Mrs. Reddington set to work immediately. Placing her confidence in her aunt, who moved in the thick of the social whirl, and a few friends that she had kept in touch with over the years, she made arrangements to introduce her daughter and niece to the ton. Vivian and Lacey soon found themselves gowned and gloved as they should be, and they—or Lacey, at least—began to feel very much at home.

Vivian was far less comfortable. Her mother had been charmed by the miracle wrought by Francois, the Parisian hairdresser she had sent for at the first possible moment after their arrival. Indeed, Mrs. Reddington had not allowed Vivian to be seen, scarcely to leave her chamber in fact, until something could be done about the ragged mess she had made of her hair. After the visit of Francois, she had emerged from her mother's dressing room with an extremely short tumble of lustrous curls framing her face, emphasizing its heart shape and the bright beauty of her eyes.

Mrs. Reddington began to see a glimmer of hope for her

ugly duckling, and she set to work with a vengeance. She had made it known to her friends that Vivian's delicate constitution had made the trip to town a difficult one for her, and so they would be obliged to allow her time to recover before venturing to accept any engagements or to receive any callers. (She had a deep regard for the truth, but she had resolved this with her conscience by concentrating on Vivian's very slender figure, not allowing herself to remember her daughter's normal rough and tumble activities at home.)

Given an extra week before Vivian officially met any members of the ton, she employed a dressmaker to advantage and drilled Vivian in the proper manners for a young lady of quality. Vivian, forcing herself to concentrate on the *Victory*, allowed herself to be made over with only an occasional explosion, while Lacey, who required no drilling, marked time impatiently, anxious to attend her first ball. She was forced to make do with chatting with their callers and occasional shopping forays with Mrs. Reddington.

Vivian retired often to her chamber to work on her manuscript, finding this a safe outlet for her emotions, and *Lord Lucifer* had begun to take shape. She had had no other glimpse of her subject before leaving home, but she had, upon reflection, formed her opinion of his character from the few times she had seen him with Ben, twice in the caves below The Lighthouse when shipments were being received and once in the taproom. He was, she knew, arrogant, very much in the habit of giving orders and having them obeyed—she could tell that even at a distance by his bearing and the manner in which the men, even Ben, snapped to attention when he spoke. She had been able to view him closely only on the occasion in the taproom, but she could recall his appearance in vivid detail—which she had recorded carefully.

She had given some thought to the reason she had not seen him on the beach the night Ben was injured—and to the reason

James Hawkins had chosen that particular night to pay an unexpected call upon his neighbors. She had not returned to The Lighthouse after visiting Ben the day after his injury. It was clear to her that her presence would only distress him, and he had quite enough on his mind. According to Joe, however, the gossip was that Hawkins was taking a tithe of the earnings of all the honest smugglers in the area.

"A tithe?" she had asked, puzzled by the old-fashioned church term.

Joe had nodded grimly. "That's what he calls it, Miss. Then he laughs and flashes those white teeth of his and says that he's like the shepherd of the local flock—and that taking only a tenth of their earnings gives them the best end of the bargain. I'll lay you odds that it won't be long before they have to pay him more than that."

Joe had looked around the stable carefully at that point, to be certain he was not overheard, then leaned toward her and continued in a still lower voice. "If you ask me, Miss, it's blasphemy, that's what it is—acting as though he has the rights of a man of the church when he's nothing but an outright thief."

"But, Joe," Vivian had asked, still puzzled, "what do they get in return for their tithe?"

"Protection," he had answered grimly.

"Protection from what? Not from the excisemen, surely."

Joe shook his head. "No, Miss. Protection from him. If they *don't* pay the tithe, they're guaranteed they'll have trouble—like old Ben Marley did. Hawkins used him as a lesson to the others."

Vivian had decided that Lord Lucifer was undoubtedly in league with James Hawkins. He too had appeared fairly recently in their part of the world, and he too was clearly involved in smuggling. That he should have been safely out of the way on the night when James Hawkins put in an appearance seemed most suspicious to her. After all, he clearly had had an investment in the shipment that was being picked up, and he had indicated that he would be present to see that it was properly taken care of. For the purposes of her story, at any rate, making them partners would work very nicely. He had looked the part of the villain and she planned to make the most of that.

Cheerfully she sat and spun her tale of smugglers and intrigue and death, mixing in the tales of spies that she had heard from Ben and Joe. Unlikely though it seemed, some of the smugglers—not Ben, of course, or any of his men—were spies for Napoleon. Traveling back and forth as frequently as they did, they were likely sources of information for the French, and some of them didn't mind picking up a bit extra for information or for delivering something beyond the usual contraband. She had been amazed by the news that there were French spies in the Bristol Channel, for it seemed too far removed from the French coast, but Ben had assured her it was true.

"And some of them be dangerous men, Miss," he had told her, "so there's another reason for you staying clear of The Lighthouse. Not many of them make their way here, but now and again one does."

Vivian had tucked the bit of information about the spies among their free traders into one of her letters to Drake, knowing that he would be surprised, too—and deeply interested. He had spent his boyhood sailing those waters, and he too, she was sure, knew many of the traders. She did not mention Ben, of course, but related it as gossip she had heard in Lynhurst. The news of James Hawkins she had already told him, but she did not add the news of his latest attempt to take over all the smuggling along the coast since it was not something that she should have been aware of.

She toyed with the idea of making Lord Lucifer a spy for the French—it seemed a likely thing for a man of no conscience and a love of adventure to do. The more she considered it, the more she liked it, for it offered a wider scope for action in her tale, and by the time dinner was served their third evening in London, Lord Lucifer was in the pay of Napoleon, and the title of her book had changed from *Lord Lucifer* to *The Spy*. No longer was he a man merely involved in making his fortune through smuggling, but a man who sent secret information to Napoleon and who occasionally carried that information to the Frenchman himself.

One afternoon as she was working on her story while awaiting yet another visit from the dressmaker, which would be followed closely by a lesson from the dancing master, the door to her chamber opened abruptly and Lacey entered unannounced, flouncing down on the bed. Vivian, in pursuit of a thought, was writing madly, balancing her little lap desk on her knees.

"What are you doing now, Vivian?" asked Lacey impatiently. "You spend more time on your scribbling than you do on any worthwhile matter—like practicing your walk or your dancing or your curtsey for court. We could at least get out and go shopping or go for a walk."

"I don't want to," returned Vivian briefly, bending over her work. "I don't like shops and I hate walking in the city, wearing little half-boots with soles so thin that they're of no practical use. They make my feet hurt. If I work on my story, I can forget for a while that I'm being held prisoner in my own home. Mama wouldn't even let me see Tom at first, until she had done with my hair and putting me in some new gowns. I wouldn't have gotten to see him at all if she hadn't needed him to practice dancing with me."

Here she paused and looked up at Lacey. "You can do all of the walking and shopping for both of us."

"That is as selfish as anything else I have ever heard you say," returned Lacey shortly. "Who am I to go out with except Aunt? We've met no one else because she doesn't think you are fit for society yet, and she spends all of her time trying to prepare you while I sit by and count the leaves on the plane tree outside my window. Do you think that no one else has anything to do with their time except take care of you?''

She turned to Vivian, who was staring at her. ''No, I thought not. You haven't given a passing thought to anyone except yourself in all of this, Vivian. You have been so caught up in what you want and what you don't want that you have made yourself quite ridiculous.''

''Who else should I be thinking of, Lacey?'' Vivian demanded. ''You? Judging by Mama's stack of invitations, you've only to wait a few more days and then you'll have more than enough routs and balls to satisfy you, and in the meantime Mama keeps buying you new gowns and trinkets and taking you out to ride in the coach. And if you think that Mama's unhappy, you're much mistaken. She's as merry as a grig, bustling about with her fashion plates from the magazines and dressing me up as though I were a doll for some little girl's nursery, so don't try to make me feel guilty about that, for it won't fly. If you need something more to do, offer to help Mama with the plans for our ball or with replying to invitations.''

Thwarted, Lacey tried another tack. ''And what about John?'' she asked coldly.

''What indeed?'' returned Vivian briskly. ''I don't see John here, do you? He isn't troubling himself about us in the least. He is perfectly content to remain at his lodge in Scotland. He doesn't think of me, so why should I think of him?''

''You are quite wrong,'' replied Lacey coldly. ''John is very interested in having you make an eligible match.''

Vivian snorted. ''I'm sure that he is—I'd be off of his hands then and he wouldn't have to spend another penny on me.''

A sudden thought struck her and she looked at Lacey curiously. ''And how would you know that he is so interested, Lacey? Have you been to a fortuneteller during your afternoon rides?''

Lacey tossed her shining yellow curls and smiled smugly. "He told me as much in this letter," she responded triumphantly, pulling a missive from her pocket and waving it in Vivian's direction.

Vivian extended her hand for it, but her cousin tucked the letter back in her pocket and patted it. "It is addressed to me, Vivian, not to you."

"And does Mama know that you have been corresponding with John?" Vivian asked sharply.

Lacey flushed a little in response, but said nothing.

"I thought as much," responded Vivian. "You are such a sneaksby, Lacey. You know how irritating Mama finds him, and yet you write to him secretly. Mama will not be pleased with you."

Lacey tossed her head. "When Aunt Lucinda thought it fit to write to Drake about your future, I thought it only right that a letter be sent to your other brother, too. It seemed the only respectful thing to do since he *is* the elder brother and the head of the family."

Vivian stared at her. "What has that to say to anything, Lacey? John already knew that we were coming to London. Mama had talked with him about it at Christmas, and naturally she has corresponded with him about opening the town house and holding a ball."

"But he did *not* know, as he put it in his letter, that 'that insufferable puppy Tom Cane would be invited to run tame in the household,'" returned Lacey, her eyes bright with malice.

"Well, of course Tom is here. Why shouldn't he be? He comes to see Mama as well as me. We've known him forever—and John only dislikes him because Tom isn't wealthy enough to marry me off to." She knew full well that the tightfisted John was reluctant to settle any money upon her and that he reasoned a wealthy man would not be bothered by her lack of fortune. So far as she had been able to discern, his greatest fear was that he would be forced to spend a considerable amount of money to persuade some gentleman to take her off his hands—or worse still, to keep her on at Trevelyan and have to pay for her out of his own pocket. It had always mystified her how a man as generous as her father had been could have sired one son so much like him in disposition and one that was so clutchfisted where others were concerned.

"But he's the only gentleman that your mama allows you to see," returned Lacey, "and you see him without always having a proper chaperone in the room with you. And you are quite right. John does not wish for a match with Tom, and so he doesn't wish you to be so much in his company."

"What utter nonsense, Eustacia!" Vivian always used Lacey's proper name when she wished to irritate her. "Tom has known me since I was in the cradle, and he's the only one I'm allowed to see because it doesn't matter a whit what Tom thinks about me and my appearance—and because Mama wants him to help me behave more fashionably. As for the thought of offering me, I'd like to see his face if it were suggested."

Here she snorted in a most unladylike manner. "Tom does think that he's all the crack, and he's told me that he's going to bring me up to snuff in no time. Drake wrote to him and to Roger Wilding and asked them to help me."

"How nice that Drake should concern himself so closely about your well-being, Vivian."

Vivian looked at her closely, brows arched knowingly. "So that is at the root of the problem, is it, Eustacia? You're green as can be because Drake has tried to look after me and has paid no attention to you!"

"Of course I'm not!" exclaimed her cousin angrily. "Although it is very like you to think so! It is nothing to me if Drake chooses to try to make a lady of you. He has no need to do the same for me because I have *always* been a lady—

never the little rudesby careening about the country that you have always been!''

Vivian grinned. ''Do you feel better now that you've tried to set me in my place? Would you like to tell me that I'm beyond help?''

Lacey did not accept the overture of peace. ''I have no need to do such a thing, Vivian,'' she replied stiffly, turning to go. ''I will say, though, that John is quite determined that Tom Cane shall not have the run of the household—and that, regardless of what Drake says, you will not be taking the *Victory* out this summer or any other time. He said it isn't ladylike and that Tom Cane would drown you both anyhow.''

Vivian's eyes grew fiery. ''You are a snake, Eustacia! How, pray tell, will brother John interfere with us while he remains in Scotland?''

Lacey smiled sweetly as she opened the door. ''Oh, didn't I mention it, Vivian? John has decided that he must put in an appearance here. He will arrive any day. I must go and tell dear Aunt about it now.''

''And I should just like to see her face when she realizes that you've gone behind her back, Eustacia. And, worse than that, if what you say is true, John will be here when our ball is given—and he and Mama will have to appear together that evening and he will try to run everything. How *very* pleased with you she will be!''

Realizing the truth of what her cousin was saying, Lacey bent over the nearby table where Vivian had stacked the pages of her manuscript and ruffled the papers angrily. ''What a waste of good paper and ink!'' she exclaimed. ''You'd best be about the business of learning to be a lady and forget about your scribbling.''

Vivian took her papers safely out of Lacey's reach and put them quietly inside her desk, turning the key. ''I think that you may need a lesson or two yourself, Lacey,'' she responded quietly.

Ignoring her comment, Lacey continued. ''Why bother to lock away your precious papers, Vivian? I suppose you are keeping a journal. Why should anyone else be interested in what happens to your or in what you think, Vivian?''

She waited for a moment, and when Vivian didn't reply, she continued. ''That's right. I didn't think that you would have considered that. There's no reason for anyone to care, you know.''

She stopped and stared intently at Vivian, who was watching her, fascinated by this sudden malicious outpouring from the normally sedate Eustacia.

''You heard me properly, Vivian! No one would give a fig about such things, you know.'' Lacey stared pointedly at Vivian's locked desk. ''Why bother to lock it when no one cares?''

Vivian took the key out of the lock of the lap desk and dropped it into her pocket, staring at Lacey but still saying nothing.

''You've always been too set upon yourself and what your opinions would mean to others. And we *don't* care, you know.'' Here Eustacia turned and sailed from the room in what she considered a very majestic manner.

Chapter Four

Mrs. Reddington was quite as vexed by the news of John's imminent arrival as Vivian had predicted. She made her feelings very clear to her niece, and Vivian was pleased to see that at least Lacey would not be held up to her as a pattern card of behavior for some time to come.

"So duplicitous!" Mrs. Reddington was heard to mutter as she glanced at her errant niece. Such phrases as "nursing a viper in one's bosom" entered frequently into her conversation, whereupon she would fix her gaze darkly upon Lacey until that young lady had the wisdom to remove herself prudently from the room.

With John safely away in the wilds of Scotland, he had not only been out of Mrs. Reddington's way, but he had also been safely employed with his hunting and fishing instead of the business of looking for a wife. Once he came to London, she greatly feared that he might suddenly settle upon some young lady, and all their lives would be altered in a twinkling. She still had not shared the news that John intended to take a bride with Vivian, feeling that it would upset her unnecessarily.

"Jealousy," explained Vivian briefly to Tom, after they had finished one of her dancing lessons and she was telling him what Lacey had done. "She wanted attention from Drake that she didn't get, so she did the next best thing—she captured his brother's interest by telling tales."

"What sort of tales?" inquired Tom with interest. He and Lacey had never gotten on together, so he was enjoying her discomfiture.

Vivian had not told him that he had played a role in their correspondence, nor that John was irritated by his presence. "Merely that I am not behaving in a becomingly ladylike manner," she shrugged.

"If he finds that shocking, he's more of a slowtop than I thought him," replied Tom, watching her inquisitively. "There's more to it than you don't mean to tell me, isn't there, Viv?"

She shrugged again and smiled. Since her arrival in London, their relationship had come closer to their old comradeship at home. While Tom still corrected her at every turn, they had somehow returned to the friendly bantering of their childhood days.

"Well, never mind," he said, dismissing the matter impatiently and returning to his primary concern. "I will be there to see that you don't disgrace yourself at the Brennans' ball tomorrow night. John will have no reason to find fault with you when he arrives in London. You dance surprisingly well, and you are beginning to look much more the thing."

Vivian curtseyed gracefully. "I am overcome by your generous compliments, sir," she replied wryly, fluttering her fan in the flirtatious manner her mother had taught her. "You are much too kind."

Tom bowed in return, but before he could reply, she had tossed her fan across the room.

"What a charade this is, Tom!" she exclaimed unhappily, collapsing onto the sofa. "How can I possibly carry on this masquerade for weeks?"

"Come now, Viv. Don't fall into a fit of the dismals now. The season doesn't last forever—and remember that at the end of that, I'll show you how to sail the *Victory.*"

"Not if John can help it," she replied bitterly. "Lacey told him about that, too, and he forbade it."

"Spiteful little cat," he said, dismissing Lacey with a wave of his hand. "Why would he forbid it?"

Forgetting in her misery to guard her tongue, she responded, "He said that it wasn't ladylike and that you would drown us both."

"He said that, did he?" demanded Tom indignantly, stung by the insult to his seamanship. "He must be thinking of his own hamfisted sailing, not mine!"

Vivian laughed in spite of herself, and he glared at her. "No, I am sorry, Tom," she said when she regained her breath. "I didn't intend to tell you that—it just slipped out. I quite depend upon you to help me, you know—and you must remember how John dislikes both of us."

Tom, his affronted dignity soothed by her apology and her clear need of his assistance, nodded thoughtfully. "No need to fret about him, though. I mean, think about it, Viv. John isn't going to stay at Trevelyan for long this summer. He never does. Once he is on his way, who's to stop us?"

Vivian brightened. "You're right, Tom," she said gratefully, squeezing his hand. "Thank you. Perhaps I will be able to live through the next few weeks when I have that to look forward to."

"Exactly so," said Tom encouragingly, glad to see that some color had returned to her cheeks.

He rose and started toward the door, then paused. "And if Drake is mad enough to risk his precious boat by allowing you to sail her—well, that's Drake's affair."

Vivian laughed and threw a pillow after him.

Gratified to see that she was herself once more, he bowed briefly and showed himself out, leaving Vivian to concentrate on the delights of summer sailing.

Happily for everyone except Lacey, John had not put in an appearance by the time she and Vivian and a host of other young women were presented at a formal drawing room at St. James the next day, and then began their round of parties. They departed for their very first ball the same evening, but John had still not sent any message announcing when to expect him. Vivian and Mrs. Reddington began to hope that perhaps he would not trouble himself by making the trip after all. John was not fond of London, nor was he particularly fond of his relatives. Taken all together, that could be enough to make him reconsider the journey.

Tom escorted the three ladies to the ball, and Roger Wilding, who had finally been allowed to call upon Vivian three days ago after her mother had decided that she was fit for social contact with outsiders, had pledged himself to dance with her that night so that they could talk of Drake. That almost gave her something to look forward to, although as she had studied Mr. Wilding at their first meeting, she could find little about him that reminded her of Drake. Her brother was always meticulous in his dress, but Mr. Wilding was much more than that. He was clearly a member of the dandy set; his cravat was intricately tied in a manner that made it well nigh impossible for him to turn his head, his waistcoat was of the daintiest buttercup yellow, and the golden tassels of his gleaming Hessians bounced jauntily as he walked.

Drake had warned her not to be put off by his dress, however, deeming him the best of all fellows and onc that she could depend upon implicitly. She had tried to bear that in mind each time she met Mr. Wilding in all of his glory, for he had called upon her each day, bringing her flowers, candy, a fan for the ball, an invitation to the theatre. "I wouldn't want Drake to think me uncivil," he explained when she had thanked him, saying there was no need for him to do so much for her.

Mrs. Reddington and Lacey were aglow at the thought of attending the ball, and the coach rang with their eager chatter. Vivian's eyes looked rather larger than usual, but they had the look of one about to be led to the stake rather than one about to embark upon an evening of pleasure.

Her expression remained much the same throughout the ball, but she was going through the motions of "doing the pretty" as Drake had bade her, when she caught a glimpse of a familiar face. The gentleman was not dancing, and he was certainly attired differently than he had been when she saw him last— but his face was unmistakable. Even in evening dress he looked forbidding, the scar on his cheek making him look more like a pirate than a gentleman of leisure.

"Who is that gentleman in the corner, the tall one with the scar?" she inquired casually of Mrs. Tavistock, one of Mrs. Reddington's friends, a partridge-plump lady encased in pink silk.

Mrs. Tavistock followed her glance and shook her head in disapproval. "That is Lord Winter," she responded in an arctic voice, "a man that you should do your best to avoid, Miss Reddington."

"Why is that, ma'am?" she asked curiously, alerted by Mrs. Tavistock's unexpected reaction.

"He is a rake, not at all fit company for a respectable young lady—no mother would allow her daughter to stand up with him," returned Mrs. Tavistock sharply.

"And so no one will dance with him? Is he an outcast, then?"

she asked hopefully, thinking immediately what a wonderful addition this would make to her story.

"Oh, there are always those that fly in the face of good sense," Mrs. Tavistock replied grudgingly. "Because he has a fortune and no wife, some are always willing to set their caps for him—but he pays no heed to them. And that just makes him all the more appealing to them—mindless chits."

"Young girls can be such fools," chimed in an elderly lady at Mrs. Tavistock's elbow. "Everyone knows that Winter takes up with only the most ineligible females—he won't have anything to do with a respectable woman."

She leaned toward Mrs. Tavistock, her thin eyebrows arched high, and murmured, "And no respectable woman would have anything to do with him. After all, everyone knows who and what he is."

Before she could continue, the rest of their group had rejoined them. Vivian didn't join in the general conversation, but covertly studied Lord Winter, who was talking with a striking dark beauty.

Vivian was entranced. Here was the subject of her latest story, ready to be studied in surroundings very different from those in which she had seen him earlier. She had no fear that he would recognize her, for she had been wearing her sailor disguise at The Lighthouse and the taproom had been dark. Whatever could he have done, she wondered, that would keep a respectable woman from associating with him? Was it a reference to the murder of his brother? Could they be referring to the smuggling?

"Whatever is *he* doing here?" asked Lacey, staring at Lord Winter over Vivian's shoulder. "Honoria Clayton pointed him out to me at the theatre last night and told me that he is simply not at *all* the thing! You wouldn't believe, Vivian, the things that they say about him!"

"I doubt half of them are true," remarked Tom Cane, who

had strolled up behind them unnoticed, "and even if they were, Lacey, you'd be just as eager as all of the other girls to stand up with him—and you'd have just as little chance of doing so. He hasn't danced with anyone yet, and I daresay he won't. He never does, you know."

"What would *you* know about it, Tom?" sniffed Lacey. "You act as though you were a regular out-and-outer instead of a scrubby schoolboy just down from Oxford."

"I know more than a niffy-naffy country miss who puts on airs to make herself interesting!" exclaimed Tom, indignant at this assault upon his dignity. "If you don't beat the Dutch, acting like you were Lady Jersey instead of Miss Eustacia Lavenham, fresh from nowhere in particular!"

Lacey's cheeks turned an unattractive shade of red and her expression boded no good for young Mr. Cane, but she shrugged nonchalantly and said in a creditably indifferent voice, "You are such a child sometimes, Tom." And she drifted away in a cloud of white to those who would appreciate her more.

Vivian grinned at him. "You really shouldn't vex her so, Tom."

Her tone was unconvincing, and Tom grinned back at her, understanding her perfectly. "Lord, Viv, I'm sure I don't know how you live with a starched-up widgeon like that. Nobody could be the pattern card of perfection that she thinks she is. Even my mother is hard pressed to think of something nice to say about her." He sounded more like her Tom with every passing day.

"What about Lord Winter, Tom?" inquired Viv casually, steering the conversation back to the subject of interest. "Do you think there's any truth in the stories about him?"

Tom looked at her sharply. "Just what stories have *you* heard about him, miss?" he demanded, once more the patronizing young gentleman. "Some of them aren't for the ears of young ladies."

"Really?" asked Vivian, wide-eyed, thinking again of her unfinished tale and hoping for ideas. "What sorts of terrible things is he supposed to have done, Tom?"

Tom looked chagrined, annoyed with himself for having brought up a matter that she obviously knew nothing about. Assuming an avuncular air, as though he were thirty years older instead of three, he tried to make the best of the situation. "Nothing that you need to know about, young lady. It is quite enough to know that he has killed his man upon several occasions."

"Oh, that!" responded Vivian, deflated. "I would have expected as much just because of the scar on his cheek. I thought perhaps there was more to it than that."

She inspected Mr. Cane's expression closely, noting that he would not meet her eyes. "And there is, isn't there, Tom?" she demanded.

He stared over her head, still refusing to meet her eyes because he knew she would read the truth there. "Nothing for your ears, Viv—so you needn't think that ripping up at me will make me tell you."

Moving closer to him, she seized his lapel. "You needn't be so toplofty, Tom Cane! You know that I can outrace you— and I still remember how you took that fence too quickly and Charger dumped you head over heels into the brook!"

"Here now, Viv!" he responded, scandalized both by her story and the damage she was doing to his new jacket. "You can't go about attacking people when they don't do just as you want them to!"

Carefully disengaging her fingers from his lapel, he eyed her with disfavor. "You are too hoydenish for town, Viv. I shouldn't wonder if you don't disgrace us all before your mama gets you safely home."

As Vivian showed every sign of renewing her grip upon his lapel, he hastened to add in a desperate whisper, "Everyone knows that Winter is suspected of being a spy for Boney. Are you satisfied now, Viv?''

Startled by his sudden revelation, she looked toward the subject of their conversation. To her astonishment, Lord Winter was looking directly at them, clearly amused by her attack upon Tom. When their eyes met, he nodded briefly to her and lifted his glass in a silent toast. Then, smiling, he turned back to his conversation with the lovely woman beside him.

''Here now, Viv! What was all that about?'' demanded Tom, scandalized by this byplay.

Annoyed by his treatment of her, Vivian lifted one shoulder nonchalantly. ''Just an admirer,'' she said casually, attempting to drift away in the same way Lacey had.

Mr. Cane grabbed her elbow, however, somewhat spoiling the effect of her drifting. ''See here, Viv,'' he said, staring down at her earnestly. ''John isn't here and Drake is in Spain, so you've no one but me to protect you.''

''I don't need anyone to look after me!'' she responded crossly, jerking her arm away from his pettishly. ''And if I did, I already have someone to do so. Drake asked Roger Wilding to look after me, and I trip over him every time I turn round!''

''Wilding!'' exclaimed young Mr. Cane, momentarily diverted. ''That Bartholomew babe? A fine lot of good he would do you. Why does your brother bother with such a frippery fellow?''

Vivian shrugged and attempted to move away, but Tom reestablished his firm grip on her elbow. ''No, you don't, Viv! Listen to me closely. You steer a wide berth from Winter, my girl. I daresay that the spying business is just a hum—but if only a half of the other stories about him are true, he's a dangerous man. And he is nothing but trouble where women are concerned. His admiration is something you don't want—

although I daresay you don't have it,'' he added frankly, thinking seriously about the matter. ''You're not at all in his style.''

Vivian jerked away pettishly. ''I wish that people would leave me alone, Tom! There is always someone telling me what to do and what no to do! I'm perfectly capable of taking care of myself!''

His derisive snort indicated his opinion of her ability to take care of herself, and she marched away indignantly, her head held high.

Chapter Five

It seemed almost too much to bear, Vivian reflected as she threaded her way through the crush of people, determined to hold back the angry tears that were almost blinding her. Mama and Lacey and John had always told her how to act and what to say. And it appeared that in London Tom had taken it upon himself to order her about just as he always had at home. Even Drake was doing so through the ubiquitous Mr. Wilding, who had offered her his services, indicating that he was willing, even eager, to squire her to any or all of her engagements.

"It will be an honor, ma'am," he had assured her earnestly. "Anything at all for dear old Drake, you know." Then, realizing that his words might be interpreted as an indication he was merely fulfilling a duty, he had hastened to add, "Eager to do so, Miss Reddington."

Here he had bent gallantly over her hand. "You may very likely set a new style, you know," he had said knowingly, nodding at her unusually short crop of curls, through which she had threaded a bandeau of a deep and vibrant crimson. It was her favorite color, a shade that Drake had always referred to by the fetching name of "turkey blood." Her gown tonight was the same vibrant shade, the sash and hem and bodice edged in gold trim.

Lacey had deeply disapproved her choice of color, observing coolly that white was much more becoming on very young ladies and pointing out that she herself would be dressed in white trimmed with silver. Mrs. Reddington too had felt that white might be more *de rigueur,* but Vivian had dug her heels in and insisted, saying that she did not wish to wear one more dull gown from the *modiste,* and that if she could not dress as she pleased, she would go home again. Her mother was far too grateful to have gotten her as far as town to risk losing her over the mere matter of wardrobe, and she had succumbed immediately. Vivian could wear what she pleased.

"After all," she had written later to Drake, "it isn't as though Vivian is selecting unbecoming gowns—it is just that they are not the usual ones worn by very young girls just entering society."

She had considered those words after she had written them and smiled, adding, "Her decision may, in fact, serve us very well. Her choices will set her apart from the other young ladies—thus far, she is just one more new face among the throng. I must admit that the more vibrant colors are most becoming to Vivian—and heaven knows that her manners will set her apart from the others. As long as they are tasteful, her gowns may as well do the same."

Vivian would have been thoroughly annoyed had she realized that her mother approved her choices. Wardrobe was the one matter about which she had been able to make her own decisions, and she was pleased to think that she was causing some small distress through her choices.

As she made her way across the crowded floor, she considered her helpless position bitterly. Everyone felt perfectly free to criticize her and tell her how to do things—even Tom. He was only a little older than she, but now he too had made it his business to order her about, all because she was in London, where she didn't want to be, doing what she didn't want to do. She had no intention of marrying, and every intention of finding a way to manage for herself without the aid of her brothers or a husband. She would sell her novel and live on the proceeds, and the devil take the consequences.

She left the crowded room for the terrace and it was there Lord Winter sought her out a few minutes later, interested in the scene he had witnessed from across the room. Still absorbed in her thoughts, she was at first unaware of his presence. Amused, he took in her flushed cheeks and darkling look as she stared out over the garden.

"An argument with your brother?" he inquired gently, his eyebrows raised.

"Tom isn't my brother!" she replied sharply, still staring out over the garden and concentrating fiercely on holding back the tears. "Although he appears to think that he is."

Not being in the habit of weeping, she was horrified to find that she was dangerously close to tears. Not for the world would she have had anyone see her in such a situation, so she did not glance up at this intruder upon her privacy, continuing to stare out over the darkened garden as though there were no sight more absorbing in all the world.

The sudden realization that she was actually expected to become engaged to some eligible party in the near future and live her life dancing to someone else's tune had caught her off guard. She might exclaim now against listening to Tom or anyone else but, once married, she knew that she would have no choice but to acknowledge her husband's right to set their course. Her lot would be to do as she was bid—something she had never been forced to do. She shook her head resolutely— she would not do so! She would think of another way!

"Indeed?" inquired Lord Winter, a little surprised. He would have sworn that they were brother and sister from the manner in which they had squared off at one another. He would have to reassess the situation. Perhaps he had witnessed a young lovers' quarrel, unlikely though it had appeared.

He was silent for a moment, positioning himself so that he could see her profile more clearly. He had noticed her immediately on the dance floor, for although she was no great beauty, her movements were graceful, her dress was arresting, and her laughter had rung out clearly at some sally her partner had made. He had noted with satisfaction that she was no simpering miss.

As he studied her now, a tear slipped down her cheek and she turned her face farther from him, acting for all the world as though she were still absorbed in studying the garden below them.

"Take my handkerchief," he said, placing it on the balustrade before her.

"No need," she replied briefly, turning her head away still more. To her horror, several companions followed the first tear and she snatched up his handkerchief, scrubbing her face furiously.

"Thank you," she said, making her voice as clear and firm as possible as she extended the damp ball of linen toward him, her gaze still fixed on the garden.

"You are most welcome," he responded courteously, eyeing the handkerchief dubiously, and finally depositing it carefully at the base of one of the potted palms that graced the terrace in honor of the occasion.

"I shan't do it!" she exclaimed ferociously.

Lord Winter looked up, surprised, and Vivian, seeing his movement from the corner of her eye, bit her lip in vexation, realizing too late that she had spoken her thoughts aloud.

"If you feel so strongly about the matter, I daresay you are quite right," he agreed courteously.

Agreeably surprised by his unexpected lack of curiosity, she continued in a passionate tone, "They expect me to marry, whether I wish to or not!"

"I see," he nodded, feeling that he was beginning to understand. "And you do not care for their choice of a husband?"

She shook her head violently, tears again threatening to overwhelm her. "They haven't chosen him! They would not dare to!"

Lord Winter stared at the back of her head, perplexed by the turn the conversation had taken. "Then perhaps I do not see," he said slowly.

Vivian, thinking suddenly of the freedom of movement accorded both of her brothers, exclaimed bitterly, "I daresay you would not! You are a man and free to do as you please— to marry or not to marry, just as you choose."

"Ah," he said softly, understanding now what she meant. "I, as you say, am most fortunate because I am able to make that decision myself—my circumstances allow it."

Vivian gave a brief, knowing nod.

"But not all men, my dear, are so fortunate," he continued smoothly.

He paused, but when she did not respond, he continued. "It is true. I myself know many who have been compelled to marry, whether they wished to or not, because they have inherited an estate but no money to care for it. It is, after all, an obligation to care for one's family, and if one must marry a lady of wealth in order to do so—so be it!"

"And I suppose the family of the young lady of wealth would wish her to marry someone with an estate and a name— even though he were impoverished."

"Just so."

Vivian shook her head. "A bargain struck at the marketplace," she said, her lip curling. "Neither one of them allowed to be a human being—each one just a piece to be bargained with."

Lord Winter shrugged. "Just so," he murmured again. "It is the way of the world."

"It is a most unsatisfactory way!" she returned sharply.

He did not reply and Vivian mulled over his observation for a minute or two. "Besides, your example doesn't fit me, sir. My family does not need to be taken care of. And I shan't allow them to tell me to marry when I don't wish to!"

"If you don't marry," he said curiously, "what will you do?"

"I shall have a little house by the sea, and ride my horse and write books and read," she said softly, staring absently into the garden. Colored lanterns lighted the spacious terrace, but the shadowy garden itself appeared to be off limits.

Following her gaze, he smiled. "I see that our hostess's garden beckons to you. May I escort you there so that you may inspect it more closely?"

Knowing full well the impropriety of his suggestion, she turned to stare at the stranger.

"You!" she exclaimed, her eyes wide.

Lord Winter was startled, but even more amused. "Yes, I believe that it is I," he responded, bowing gracefully.

"Well, that isn't what I meant, of course," she responded tartly, annoyed by his amusement.

"Have we met, my dear?" he asked, staring down at her. Upon closer inspection, the child was much more appealing than he had at first thought. Not a beauty, of course, but vivid and warm—and her dark eyes were very fine indeed. "I feel that I would remember it, had we done so."

"No, of course not," she said hurriedly, remembering the circumstances—and Ben. "But, of course, everyone knows you, Lord Winter," she added ingenuously.

He laughed a little dryly. "I believe that you are right, my dear—and I fear that you have heard nothing to my credit."

Since this was undeniably true, Vivian was momentarily at a loss for a response. Lord Winter, thoroughly enjoying the moment despite the brief stab of bitterness, watched her think desperately and then reply.

"I know that all of the young ladies wish to dance with you," she responded happily, pleased that she could say something that was both inoffensive and true.

"I was not aware of that," he replied with great untruth, "but if that is indeed the case, would *you* care to dance with me, ma'am? Or would you prefer a stroll in the garden?"

"Neither!" announced Tom from behind them. He stood in the doorway, the picture of quivering indignation. Holding out his hand to Vivian, he said, "I believe that you were going to dance with me now, Viv."

Exactly what one would expect of Tom, she thought to herself indignantly. He thought that he could tell her just what to do and that she would do it.

"Our dance is later, Tom," she replied frigidly. Turning to Lord Winter, she smiled and her voice warmed. "And I would love to take that stroll in the garden now, sir."

Well aware that he was being used, but delighted by the lift of her chin as she turned her back on the horrified Tom, Lord Winter entered into the charade with alacrity. Offering her his arm, they strolled down the steps to the darkness of the garden, leaving Tom, who suddenly felt the need for reinforcements, to search out the previously despised Mr. Wilding to form a rescue party and invade the garden.

"Excuse me for mentioning this, my dear," he said lazily as they entered the darkness of the garden, "but, while you appear to know my name, I am not yet in possession of yours—except that your given name is apparently Vivian. A charming name, I might add."

Vivian felt herself flushing. Why should it matter to her whether he found her name charming or not? Forcing herself to be casual and pleasant, she smiled and said, "Forgive me, Lord Winter. My name is Vivian Reddington."

He stopped, turned toward her, and bowed, taking her hand as he did so. "It is my very great pleasure to make your acquaintance, Miss Reddington," he said softly.

Without her knowing precisely how it happened, he had also pulled her toward him very gently and lifted her hand to his lips.

It was at this inauspicious moment that Tom and Mr. Wilding arrived upon the scene, wheezing but determined to bear her away. Lord Winter was not surprised by their sudden appearance, but he was exceedingly amused—and amusement was something that he had found to be in short supply during recent years.

"May I be of some service to you, gentlemen?" he drawled.

Ignoring him, Tom reached over and took Vivian's arm, prepared to guide her back to the lights of civilization, but she pulled away from him.

"Just what do you think you're doing, Tom Cane?" she demanded angrily.

"I'm taking you back inside where you should be," he said in a low voice. "If you had the sense that God gave a goose, you wouldn't be out here now, kicking up such a dust that people will take note of it if you don't take care."

"Not a goose," protested Mr. Wilding. "Not the kind of thing likely to persuade a young lady, Mr. Cane."

He executed a brief bow in the direction of Vivian and Lord Winter. "I would be honored, Miss Reddington, if you would allow me the next dance."

Before Vivian could reply, Lord Winter smiled down at her. "Had you not promised this dance to me, ma'am?" he inquired lightly, offering her his arm.

Taking it firmly, she smiled up at him. "Thank you, sir. I had almost forgotten." And nodding in the general direction of the other two gentleman, she turned toward the terrace.

The ensuing scene was as memorable as Tom and Mr. Wilding had feared it would be. They were in time to see Lord Winter lead her onto the floor, and to note the ripple of movement in the room as heads turned and the whispering began.

"Who's the little filly with Winter?" Tom heard one florid-faced man inquire in a loud voice.

"Don't know," responded his companion, holding up his glass and staring at Vivian, "but I daresay everyone here will know within the next few minutes."

Tom groaned and shook his head. "That headstrong little fool."

Mr. Wilding cleared his throat and nodded. "She's set them all in a bustle," he agreed unhappily. "No two ways about it."

He watched them for a moment, then added in a tone unusually aggrieved for one of his easygoing temperament, "Drake told me that she would bear watching, but I didn't realize just what the old fellow meant. He should have warned me that she'd be the very deuce to look after."

Tom nodded in agreement and, bound by their mutual affliction, they lapsed into a gloomy silence as they watched their charge become the focal point of interest in the ballroom.

For the moment, Vivian was happily unaware that they were being scrutinized. As the music started, she moved lightly through the figures of the dance, concentrating on the steps, determined not to make a spectacle of herself.

Lord Winter watched her, enjoying both her earnestness and her lack of pretense. "You dance very well, Miss Reddington," he said, locking his arm through hers as they turned.

"Thank you, sir," she replied, smiling up at him. "Tom will be gratified to know that he taught me well. I am afraid he quite despaired of ever doing so. It was only last week that he informed me that my pony could dance as well as I."

His eyes lit with laughter at this sally, but his expression remained grave. "I should hope that you took him to task for such a lapse in manners, Miss Reddington."

"Not at all," she responded. "If I were to take Tom to task for each lapse of manners, I should never have time to do anything else. Aside from which," she added, determined to be fair, "he was quite right, you know. Last week Pimm *could* have danced as well as I."

Lord Winter's shoulders shook, causing those closest to them to stare even more curiously. He was not a man noted for his good humor.

"I had not expected to enjoy myself tonight, my dear," he remarked lightly, as the movements of the dance brought them together once more. "Thanks to you, however, this has been a most delightful evening."

Suddenly she was sharply aware of his nearness, of the strength of his arm locked through hers as he swung her round, of the warmth of his glance as he laughed down at her, and she was grateful to be returned to her place so that she could regain her composure. She had felt no such reaction with Tom or any of the other young men with whom she had danced, and she was dismayed to discover that she was eagerly anticipating the next movement of the dance that would bring them together.

Her first assessment of him had been right. He was indeed a most dangerous man.

Chapter Six

The ride home in the carriage that evening was a memorable one. The instant the carriage door had closed behind them, Tom delivered his opinion of her behavior, warning her of its possible severe consequences: at the very least, the ladies whose approval she needed would not call upon her and she would not receive the coveted voucher for Almack's.

"If they don't care for me, then I don't care for them!" she had exclaimed, her tone quite as angry as his. "Why should I care what those strangers think of me?"

"Because they will determine whether you are accepted by the rest of the ton," he had replied, attempting to speak in a calm, rational voice to one that he clearly considered to be teetering upon the brink of lunacy. "Because if they decide to cut you, Vivian, you may as well go home to Trevelyan right now."

Vivian opened her mouth to reply, but paused. To her amazement, she realized that she did not want to go home just yet. Now that she had met Lord Lucifer, she wanted the opportunity to study him at close range. He should provide the inspiration she needed to complete her book. She could not, of course, mention her reason, since the family had no idea what she was working on. So she shrugged her shoulders indifferently and made a face at Tom. "Perhaps going home is a good idea," she replied coolly, knowing full well that she would do no such thing.

"You *would* think so!" exclaimed Lacey bitterly, who had been brooding over her grievances in the corner. "It's just as I told you the other day—you give no thought to anyone else's feelings or desires. *I,* for instance, would like to stay in London, not go back to be buried alive in the country. *I* would like to receive callers and have a voucher for Almack's—but do you spare a thought for me? Of course not!"

"Don't be such a ninny, Lacey," returned Vivian. "Why should you not have callers and receive a voucher?"

"Because *you* are Miss Reddington of Trevelyan, Vivian. As Tom so kindly put it, I am 'Miss Eustacia Lavenham of nowhere in particular.' "

Tom looked uncomfortable and Mrs. Reddington said in a disapproving tone, "That was really not very well done of you, Thomas." Turning to her niece, she added kindly, "And of course it isn't true, Lacey."

"It may not be true, but it might as well be, Aunt," she said acidly. "If Vivian makes herself an outcast, who will chaperone me to all of the routs? You will be occupied with Vivian, possibly even having to take her back to Trevelyan. I would have no choice but to come with you."

"Nonsense!" said Mrs. Reddington briskly, to everyone's surprise.

She had at first been horrified by her daughter's flouting of decorum but, upon reflection, she was secretly exultant that Vivian had attracted the attention of such a notably hardened case as Lord Winter. So far as she could tell, no real harm had been done, but everyone present at the ball was now aware of the identity of Miss Vivian Reddington and of the fact that Lord Winter had singled her out. They would call and, providing Vivian did nothing truly disreputable in the foreseeable future, she would become a focal point of interest for at least a few days and would doubtlessly receive her voucher for the exclusive Almack's in record time. Her mother's most pressing concern was whether or not Vivian should wear the same color combination to their next ball, which would be the following evening.

"No one will be going home to Trevelyan because of this," she said confidently. "You mark my words!"

And her prediction proved true. The next day their drawing room was crowded with visitors, both well-wishers and the envious, and Vivian, who was not accustomed to being the center of attention, was rather overwhelmed by it all. Lacey, whose beauty had always drawn attention in any group, even in the backwaters of Lynhurst, received an occasional glance and comment, but it was clear that the interest of the visitors was focused on Vivian. Just why a miss fresh from the schoolroom should appeal to the notorious Lord Winter, enough to draw him onto the dance floor, was a subject hotly debated in many clubs and drawing rooms that day, and many wished to meet her so that they could form their own opinions.

One of the first to take possession of the drawing room that morning was Mr. Earl Darroway, a cheerful rattlepate who had been the first to solicit her hand for a dance after she had stood up with Lord Winter. Mr. Darroway prided himself upon being fashionable and, as he had told Vivian the evening before, he could see right away that she was going to be all the rage.

"Nacky notion of mine," he had confided, "to be the first to pay my respects. Always wanted to set a fashion myself, but nothing ever took—not even my lemon-striped waistcoat. Next best thing to setting a fashion is to pay court to someone who will—and you will, you know," he added helpfully, seeing that Vivian was having some difficulty following his train of thought. "Thought so the moment I saw you with Winter."

"Oh, I shouldn't think so, Mr. Darroway," she responded in amazement. "Whatever would make you believe such a thing?"

"Look at 'em," he returned, casually indicating with a lift of his brow a group of ladies gathered at the edge of the dance floor. "They are watching every move you make, ma'am. And tomorrow half of 'em will go out and have their hair cut short and look for fabric the color of the gown you're wearing—all in the hope that Winter will ask them to stand up with him."

Vivian was wide-eyed, finding it very difficult to believe what she was hearing. "Is he so much admired, then?" she asked, eager to hear more of her subject.

Mr. Darroway considered her question a moment, then shook his head. "Not admired—no, couldn't say that at all. But he's one of a kind, you know, not just a top-sawyer or a devil with his fives—though he is, of course. But that don't matter to him. Matter of fact, can't say that anyone or anything matters to him. He's a bad man. Killed his brother for the title, you see."

"Then why would anyone wish to have his admiration?" she asked, puzzled.

Mr. Darroway wrestled with her question for a moment, then shook his head. "He's a bad man—the devil himself, some say—but he's still good ton. Good family, you know, and money, and style. And he don't care for anyone, and that seems to work magic on most people. Some of the young cubs always try to act like him and dress like him."

He nodded toward a very young man, dressed all in black, except for an immaculate white shirt and white pique waist-coat—the image of Lord Winter, from the bored expression to the casual pose. "Teddy Graham," he said. "Thinks he's quite the thing. Works out at Gentleman Jackson's and drives a curricle with two showy grays. The silly chub oversets it regularly, but he thinks he's all the go—just like Winter. Only he ain't, of course. Probably break his neck before the year is out.''

Vivian had mentally filed away all of the information about Lord Lucifer, pleased to be gathering more for her book, and she had not been surprised when Mr. Darroway was the first of her guests that morning. What had surprised her was the number of visitors who came to call, most of them quite unknown to her.

She was chatting with Mr. Darroway and Mr. Wilding, glad to be with two that she at least knew, when a sudden silence fell over the room. Glancing up, they saw the reason: Lord Winter was standing in the doorway. Mr. Darroway glanced at her knowingly, and she understood at once what he meant. Winter had taken full command of the room simply by appearing.

Glancing toward a low table at a huge bouquet of hothouse roses the color of the gown Vivian had worn the evening before, he made his way to her and bowed. ''I am pleased to see that they arrived, ma'am,'' he said, nodding at the roses.

''They are lovely, Lord Winter,'' replied Vivian with a smile.

''The shade was difficult to find, Miss Reddington,'' he said seriously, although his eyes glinted. ''Turkey blood is apparently considered a very singular shade of red.''

Those listening to the conversation exchanged puzzled glances, but Vivian's laugh rang through the drawing room. When he had admired the shade of her gown the evening before, she had told him what she and Drake had always called it, and had regaled him with stories from their childhood, including her thwarted attempt to run away with the gypsies.

Mrs. Reddington, who had been watching the present exchange nervously, allowed herself to breathe again. Perhaps

Vivian would not do anything outrageous after all—and Lord Winter was conducting himself as a gentleman should.

In truth, that gentleman had gone to the ball the evening before with every intention of leaving early an affair that he knew would be insipid, having been drawn there only because of a business matter. To his surprise, he had enjoyed himself—and the reason was Miss Reddington. She and her friends had amused him—just as Tom Cane and Roger Wilding were amusing him now. From the corner of his eye he could see young Mr. Cane, his face scarlet with indignation at this appearance of the wolf within the hen house, while Mr. Wilding, saucereyed, was taking it all in but clearly wishing himself elsewhere. Lord Winter had no intention of allowing such pleasure to slip through his fingers—and the first step in his campaign was to secure the approval of Vivian's mother.

So attentive was he, in fact, as he seated himself beside Mrs. Reddington, that she became quite captivated. When the last of their callers had been ushered to the door, she announced to the family group that he was most truly a gentleman.

"Why, his manners are faultless," she told them. "I cannot help but believe that people are merely jealous of his position and his wealth and so they gossip more than they should. I am certain that those awful stories about him cannot be true!"

"Everyone knows that he's a murderer!" snapped Lacey, annoyed because Lord Winter had all but ignored her, even when she had made her most appealing overtures. "You think that, Aunt, simply because he spent his time making up to you!"

"And you're cross as crabs because he didn't even notice you!" returned Tom. But he was not at all pleased by the fact that Lord Winter had chosen to call upon them.

"He might as well announce to the world that he means to pursue his interest in you, Viv," said Tom gloomily. "They will be making wagers about you in all the clubs, if they haven't already begun it.''

Mr. Wilding nodded in his head unhappily. ''Bound to, I'm afraid. Too great an interest in Winter, you know, and he hasn't danced with a young lady in years. And now to top it off, he's come to call. Winter don't pay calls. People are bound to talk.''

He rested his chin thoughtfully upon the head of his ornate malacca walking stick. He saw deep waters ahead and envisioned himself trying to explain to Drake how he had allowed his little sister to become the talk of the town and the recipient of the attentions of such a notorious rake while under his protection. The mere thought of it made him begin to consider the wisdom of a little rural refreshment at his quiet country estate for a protracted period of time—preferably until the news was borne to him that young Miss Reddington was safely back at *her* country home.

A more cheerful thought struck him, however, and, not being of a particularly reflective turn of mind, he shared it immediately. ''Perhaps it's only a freak,'' he said happily.

The others stared at him for a moment, not following his line of thought. Few people did, so Mr. Wilding was not put off by this reaction.

''Perhaps he don't really mean anything by the attention,'' he explained kindly for those less swift in intellectual exercise. ''Very likely he only did it for the sport of it, you know—standing up with Miss Reddington as he did.''

Vivian, having followed Mr. Wilding's intellectual endeavors, sat a little straighter, her eyes a little brighter. ''Do I understand you to say, Mr. Wilding,'' she said slowly, ''that Lord Winter might have been making sport of me in front of all those people?''

Recognizing immediately that he had made a mistake, Mr. Wilding hastened to retrieve his error. ''Not making sport of you, no, of course not—a deuced ungentlemanly thing to do—

not but what many take leave to doubt that Winter *is* a gentle-man—''

Seeing by her expression that he had made yet another blunder, Mr. Wilding hurried desperately on, hoping to strike safe ground at last. ''What I mean to say is that he might not have considered the awkwardness of your position, Miss Reddington. Very accustomed to doing things his own way, Winter is. Very likely just came all over him that he wished to dance, and he thought that you would make a delightful partner . . .'' Here he bowed in Vivian's direction, hoping that this compliment would appease her.

''And I suppose that if my grandmother had been standing there when he decided that he must dance, he would have stood up with her?'' she inquired, her voice mild.

Mr. Wilding appeared to struggle with this question a moment, then gave way. ''Perhaps not your grandmother,'' he said doubtfully, ''because it seems to me that Drake told me that you haven't any grandparents still living. So naturally—''

''In the name of all that's holy, Wilding, will you stop rattling on?'' demanded Tom, who had borne all that he could without speaking. ''Naturally, she didn't really mean that Winter would have danced with her grandmother! Viv just meant that *you* meant to say that Winter would have stood up with anyone.''

Mr. Wilding looked relieved. ''Glad to hear you didn't think he would have stood up with your grandmother,'' he said, nodding at Vivian as though relieved by this evidence of her good sense. ''Not the thing to do, especially when your grand-mother—''

He was cut short by the exasperated Tom. ''What is important, Viv, is that you not make a spectacle of yourself by allowing Winter to single you out!''

''Indeed?'' she inquired, her voice chilly. ''And what if I enjoy his attentions?''

"Then you are a pea-goose!" he announced frankly. "But I don't think that we'll really have to worry about the matter. I daresay that come tomorrow Winter will have forgotten all about this and be giving his attention elsewhere."

Unfortunately for Mr. Wilding and Tom, however, this was only the beginning of their distress, for Lord Winter had decided to pay very particular attention to Vivian—and he demonstrated that at the ball they attended that very evening.

No sooner had Tom settled his group of ladies comfortably that evening than Lord Winter appeared to claim Vivian for the next dance. There was nothing to be done about it, for Mrs. Reddington relinquished her daughter with a smile, much to Mr. Cane's disgust.

"You know what this means, ma'am," he said grimly, watching as Vivian smiled up at her partner.

"Why, of course I do, Tom dear," she replied, smiling. "It means that Vivian has captured the attention of one of the most notable men in London, a gentleman who hasn't given the time of day to a young lady for years."

Tom snorted inelegantly. "A gentleman! We must be speaking of two different men, ma'am! *I* am referring to Lord Winter—a man with a reputation that is highly questionable at best!"

"Don't be such an old woman, Tom," replied Mrs. Reddington blithely. "That is merely gossip, and you know it. Why, if this hadn't happened, Vivian might very well have been standing and watching others dance instead of having her card filled."

"Like me, do you mean, Aunt?" inquired Lacey acidly. "Perhaps if I had chosen to make a spectacle of myself, I too might be engaged for every dance."

Diverted by this comment from the enemy, Tom forgot his annoyance with Vivian for a moment. "I don't think it likely,

Lacey," he responded briskly. "After all, it wasn't Vivian that singled out Lord Winter, it was the other way about, if you recall. I didn't notice him giving you the time of day."

"And it's as well that he did not!" returned Lacey, flushing angrily. "I would certainly have never put my family to the blush by behaving in such a manner! Why, I can imagine what John will have to say when—"

Catching her aunt's eye, she halted abruptly, recalling too late that this was not a happy turn for the conversation to be taking. Excusing herself hastily, she moved to the side of a young lady whose acquaintance she had made at last night's ball.

Tom and Mrs. Reddington watched her go. "She does beat the Dutch!" he exclaimed. "She can't bear to see Viv receiving any attention at all, let alone the lion's share of it."

He grinned at Mrs. Reddington, forgetting his aggravation for the moment in his pleasure at seeing Lacey get her comeuppance. "I never thought I'd see the day when Viv would manage to upstage Eustacia."

"Nor I," replied her mother, a satisfied smile playing over her lips. "Now if we can just keep Vivian from doing anything too outrageous for a few days, we can use this to our advantage very nicely. She has the attention of all the young men of the ton."

"I am afraid that she does," agreed Mr. Wilding ruefully, and the other two looked up, startled, not having realized he was standing so close. "Just been round to White's and the odds are very high."

"The odds on what?" demanded Tom. "What are they wagering on?"

"That Winter will drop her by the end of the week. They say that he has never sustained any interest for longer than two weeks even in a high flyer—and it is less than that for any proper young woman."

"I thought he never showed an interest in respectable women!" exclaimed Tom.

"Not in years," agreed Mr. Wilding. "But the last two times he did—all a very long time ago—neither of them lasted longer than a week."

Mrs. Reddington turned a worried eye to the dance floor, where Vivian was now dancing with one of the young men who had waited patiently. She did not look as though she were enjoying it particularly, but she was at least dancing gracefully.

"That would be terrible, Tom," she murmured. "Worse than having him show any interest at all. Imagine the humiliation."

"He had better not be trifling," returned Tom indignantly, forgetting for the moment that he had been protesting her having anything to do with Winter at all. And the three of them watched Vivian intently, willing Winter to put in another appearance.

They were no more anxious than Vivian herself. She had not thought to enjoy Lord Winter's company—he was, after all, the villain of her book, but he was much more amusing than she had imagined a gentleman capable of being. Many a lady more experienced than she had fallen prey to his charm.

When he reclaimed her for a dance later in the evening, she smiled in relief, her pleasure in seeing him clear.

"Bored?" he asked sympathetically.

"Not any longer," she answered ingenuously. "You do not try to impress me or talk about matters that I care nothing for."

He smiled down at her. "You do me too much honor, ma'am."

She shook her head and chuckled. "It is the truth, Lord Winter. You may believe me."

She glanced in the direction of a young gentleman in a cherry-colored waistcoat. "Mr. Westcott looks and behaves very much like one of my spaniels at home," she said in a low voice. "Bones always waits for a pat on the head, staring at you until you give way and give him the attention he requires."

"And did you give Mr. Westcott the attention *he* required?" asked Lord Winter in amusement.

She shook her head. "I could not bring myself to encourage him," she confessed. "He was reciting some of his own poetry, and it was decidedly wretched verse."

"I assure you that I shall spare you that much," he said blandly. "Should I take it into my head to recite poetry, I swear that I shall consult you for your favorites. I would not inflict upon you any that I have written myself."

"Do you write poetry?" she asked, startled.

"No longer," he assured her. "It is a disease that afflicts only young men unless they truly are poets, so you are quite safe. Although . . ."

Vivian looked up curiously to see what had caused him to pause. To her surprise, he was gazing down at her with an intensity that made her catch her breath.

"Although what?" she asked, smiling.

"Although you almost make me wish that I were young again," he said smoothly.

She shook her head. "I don't believe that's what you were going to say, Lord Winter," she said reprovingly, "although you recovered very nicely."

He laughed, to the great interest of those watching. "How very observant you are, Miss Reddington. I shall have to be more careful."

She nodded. "It's one of my few qualities, I'm afraid. Drake always said that I noticed everything that was going on at home."

"While I cannot allow you to say that you have few qualities, I would most certainly agree with your brother. Perhaps you should offer your assistance to the Bow Street Runners."

Her eyes brightened at the mention of the Fieldings' famous

Runners. "It would be interesting," she agreed enthusiastically. "I have always thought that I could do that kind of thing very well."

Lord Winter looked mildly alarmed. "I did not mean, of course, that you should join them, Miss Reddington."

"No, I could not, naturally," she sighed in agreement. "Being a woman is so very tiresome."

"Perhaps you will grow reconciled in time," he replied soothingly.

She shook her head. "Time will make no difference. Only discovering a way to take care of myself through my stories without depending on my brothers or a husband will make a difference."

He looked at her curiously. "Are you so determined to do so? I fear that will be a very difficult matter, Miss Reddington."

She nodded and sighed. "I know."

He glanced about the room, noting all of the watchful faces. "It is too bad that you cannot discover a way to bank the curiosity of those about you," he said in amusement.

"What do you mean, sir?" she asked, her attention caught.

"There is not a person in this room who would not like to know more about you," he said lightly. "They are watching your every move."

She shook her head. "They are watching you."

"I have been called a proud man, Miss Reddington, but I hope that I won't offend you when I say they are watching you because they have seen that I am interested in you—and that is a most unusual matter. Like you, I am usually bored by affairs like this."

She thought about this carefully. "I am afraid, though, that I see no way to take advantage of their interest—not in any way that will help me with my problem."

Lord Winter's shoulders shook slightly, but he hid his amusement skillfully. "I see that you do not intend to add to my self-consequence, ma'am."

Recalled abruptly from her thoughts about her problem, she stared at him for a moment, puzzled, then a smile brightened her eyes. "Do you mean that I should be impressed because you are interested in me, Lord Winter?" she inquired.

He nodded, his smile deepening.

"But there is no reason to be, for I know that you don't belong here either. All of this bores you just as it does me—so we are entertaining each other."

He bowed. "You are right, of course," he responded lightly, taking her hand and lifting it to his lips. "And I shall miss seeing you for the next few days. I trust that you will find something to hold your interest for that time."

"Are you leaving, then?" she asked, disappointed at the thought. Knowing that she would be spending time with him had made this second evening of dancing palatable; without his presence, the routs they attended would seem insipid.

"I am afraid that I must—business calls. But I will be back very shortly," he assured her, "and I shall call as soon as I return."

At the mention of business, her thoughts turned immediately to smuggling. It seemed less enjoyable now—Lord Lucifer the villain had somehow become Lord Winter her friend. She looked at him sharply, thinking of Ben and wondering if she could have been right about Lord Lucifer's connection with James Hawkins.

"Is there something wrong, Miss Reddington?" he asked, noting her expression.

She shook her head and turned away lightly. "No, of course not, Lord Winter." She looked over her shoulder and smiled. "But I shall miss you."

He bowed and watched her rejoin her group, then made his apologies to his hostess and left. He sat a long time before his fire that evening instead of retiring early to prepare for his journey as he had intended. Vivian's face rose before him in the flames and again he saw her smile. It had been a very long time since someone had missed him.

Chapter Seven

Tired though she was, Vivian did not go to bed immediately either. Instead, she sat in her nightgown and read through her story, revising portions as she wrote. Lord Lucifer was now a curious blend of hero-villain, but quite a charming character. Before meeting him in London, the motive she had given Lucifer for murdering his brother in the novel had been greed. Taking her pen, she marked through those pages. The idea of that murder unsettled her, for she now associated Lord Lucifer too much with Lord Winter, and she had difficulty imagining his doing such a thing, regardless of what she had heard about him. She had been unnerved by what Tom had told her about his being suspected of spying for Napoleon. She had congratulated herself for adding that to the story herself, never dreaming that there could be some element of truth in it. In her story, Lucifer had slain his elder brother because he wanted his wealth and title and because his brother had discovered that he was a spy, and was going to turn him in to the authorities. Busily she marked an "X" through the pages that were most incriminating.

The man she had met in London was too charming a man to be a murderer and a spy.

When she went to bed that morning, exhausted by her revisions, which had eliminated most of her novel, she was too tired to bother with locking the manuscript away. When Lacey came to awaken her, the pages still lay scattered on her desk. Instead of waking her immediately, Lacey seated herself quietly, curious to see what Vivian had been about in her writing, and read as quickly as she could. She did not have time to finish it all, but she recognized Lord Lucifer—and smiled.

"Aunt asked me to tell you it is almost time to leave, Vivian," Lacey said quietly, shaking her cousin's shoulder after placing the pages exactly where they had been.

Vivian's eyes fluttered open, and then she remembered her work. Glancing quickly at her desk and then at Lacey, she said, "Tell her that it will take me only a few minutes to dress and I will join you."

"It should take you longer than that to prepare yourself," observed Lacey disapprovingly. "You don't wish to look thrown together in just any skimble-skamble fashion." And she closed the door sharply to emphasize her opinion.

Vivian dressed quickly and locked her manuscript carefully away. As she started down the steps, she could hear the bustle of arrival below her, and her heart sank as she looked down into the face of her disapproving brother.

"Hello, John," she said in a flat voice, enthusiasm notably lacking.

"Vivian." He nodded briefly, lifting his glass to his eye to study her costume more closely. "Not particularly the thing for a young girl to wear, is it?" he inquired shortly, eyeing the dark flowered frock and the claret-colored pelisse she wore over it.

"But very fetching, don't you think?" returned Mrs. Reddington briskly. "Hurry along, Vivian. It is past time for us to be at Sally Hilton's breakfast. I'm sure your brother needs a little time to unpack and go round to his club.''

Mentioning his club suddenly brought to mind the wagers on Vivian, however, and she changed her tactics immediately. ''On the other hand, John, it has been this age since you have been to London and seen anyone. I'm certain that Sally would have invited you had she known that you were to be in town— indeed, it would have been thoughtful to let *me* know that you were going to be in town,'' she inserted darkly, remembering her grievance against Eustacia and her son. ''I daresay you thought that merely letting Lacey know would be adequate. I sometimes wonder where I went amiss in rearing you, John.''

''My cousin appears to be aware of her obligation to the head of the family, ma'am,'' he said coldly. ''I wish that as much could be said of others.''

''And I suppose you mean that for me,'' said Mrs. Reddington sharply. ''Do remember that you are speaking to your mother, John, and not to one of your minions!''

He gave her a brief bow. ''I shall try to bear that in mind, ma'am, if you will remember that I bear the responsibility for what happens to the members of this family.''

''You appear to have a very convenient memory,'' she sniffed. ''The only time you leave your beloved Scotland is when you want something or when you mean to be unpleasant. Your sense of responsibility seems to overtake you only when it suits you.''

Before he could reply to this, she turned to Vivian and Eustacia, who were waiting uneasily by the door. ''The carriage is waiting, girls. We must be going.'' And with a brief nod, she hurried them out the door, leaving the affronted John.

As their carriage bowled briskly away, her anger subsided and Mrs. Reddington began to regret her outburst. Undoubtedly John would go to his club, learn of the wager about his sister, and come home in a fury. At least, however, Tom and Mr.

Wilding had not been calling for them that morning and Lord Winter was out of town. Having any of those gentlemen appear while John was there would have set the cat among the pigeons with a vengeance. Settling back against the cushions, she sighed. They would just have to face matters as they arose— and she put all thought of her troublesome son to one side for the moment and prepared to enjoy the breakfast. Mrs. Reddington had learned early in her marriage the skill of enjoying the present moment and putting aside worrisome problems. They would still be waiting when she had time to attend to them, and if they weren't, so much the better that she had not wasted her time with them.

Tom and Mr. Wilding, along with a host of admirers, paid their respects to Vivian at the breakfast, once more leaving Lacey with her nose out of joint since she only received a tiny portion of the attention. After things settled down, Vivian found herself singled out by the handsome woman she had seen with Lord Winter on the first night she danced with him. Introducing herself as Lady Connaught, the widow of an Irish nobleman, she asked Vivian to take a turn with her in the garden. Curious to learn anything more she could about Lord Winter—and just as curious to know why this extremely lovely woman wished to speak with her—Vivian agreed with alacrity.

"You must forgive my being so forward, my dear," said Lady Connaught with a smile, "but I saw you dancing with Richard at the ball the other night, so I feel as though we have a link between us."

"Richard?" inquired Vivian. "Do you mean Lord Winter?"

Lady Connaught gave a low laugh. "Forgive me, I should have been more formal, Miss Reddington, but I have known him so long, you see, and I quite forgot that you have only just met him." And she looked questioningly at Vivian, who nodded.

"Yes, that was the first time I had met him." And she paused, hoping against hope that Lady Connaught would tell her more about Lord Winter. Nor was she disappointed.

"Of course, I should have realized. But I have known him for such a very long time, you see. Why, I was no older than you are now when he fell in love with me."

Vivian looked at her quickly, not entirely surprised by what she was saying, but wondering just why she was being told.

Lady Connaught, mistaking the meaning of her glance, nodded. "He said that he could not help himself," she said complacently. "One glance at me as we were dancing—with different partners, of course—and he said he knew immediately that he could never regard another woman as beautiful." She laughed a little at the memory, then sighed.

Vivian, who had been studying the other woman's face, could find no fault with this statement. Lady Connaught was indeed a beauty, her hair as glossy and dark as the wing of a blackbird, her skin as creamy and fresh as that of a young girl.

"I can see why he would think so," she said sincerely, making a mental note that she would fit Lady Connaught into her new novel. Now that she had laid aside *The Spy,* she needed a new project. "I am sure that I have seen no one in London who could hold a candle to you."

The widow glanced at her sharply. She was accustomed to being regarded by other ladies with jealousy—or sometimes with disdain—but not with such open admiration.

"Poor Richard," she continued, "I would give anything if he could forget me and finally marry. I beg him to do so—but he does not seem able to forget me. He told me—" Here she paused and looked delightfully self-conscious. "He told me that I am his first love and his last."

Vivian wondered privately why he should remain unhappy, since the lady was now a widow, but politeness forbade her to place the question directly. Lady Connaught, satisfied with her work, soon departed, leaving Vivian to mull over this latest bit of the puzzle of Lord Winter. Instead of suffering from the jealousy that Lady Connaught had hoped to inspire, however, Vivian was fascinated by this latest piece in the puzzle of the enigmatic Lord Winter. When she was still working on *The Spy,* she had toyed with the idea of giving Lord Lucifer a broken heart, but she had not been able to reconcile that notion either with Lord Lucifer or with Winter, the careless man who chatted so easily with her and seemed to care for no one.

A further inquisition of Tom revealed that he had indeed almost married when he was younger, but the young woman had married someone else. Since the wagering had begun, more talk about Winter's past had circulated, and Tom made it his business to hear all of it. She also discovered from Tom that Winter had once possesssed an older brother and it was indeed rumored, just as she had heard back at The Lighthouse, that Winter had been responsible for his brother's death. Despite this confirmation of the smuggler's information, however, she had not been able to convince herself that he could actually be a murderer. Unfortunately, she had been able to find out little more about his dead brother, although she had instructed Tom to find out what he could.

She rode home from the breakfast that day in a very thoughtful frame of mind, but that did not last for very long. She had no more than taken off her bonnet when a maid appeared to summon her to the study to see her brother. Sighing, she ran her fingers through her curls and prepared to meet him. He had already been angry about Tom, and doubtless Lacey had now informed him about Lord Winter. She did not look forward to speaking with John at the best of times, and she was certain that this would be far from the best.

John stood with his back to the fireplace, his hands clasped behind him. When she entered the room, he said nothing, but merely studied her in what he clearly considered an intimidating manner. Vivian's eyes did not waver from his, however, and he finally averted his gaze and cleared his throat importantly.

"It has come to my attention, Vivian, that—" he began, speaking in a solemn, measured voice, but he was not allowed to finish.

"That I have been seeing Tom Cane and, far worse than that, that I have danced with the notorious Lord Winter and doubtless played the very deuce with any opportunity that I had for making an eligible match—except of course that I had virtually no opportunity of making an eligible match."

Vivian seated herself easily in a comfortable chair and gazed up at him questioningly. "Have I missed any point you wished to make, John?" she inquired sweetly.

John glared at her for a moment. "Only one," he said quietly, determined not to lose his temper with Vivian. She had always known precisely how to go about upsetting him, and he was determined that she would not overset him this time.

"And what may that be?"

"That I prefer that my sister not drag our name through the mud by making her behavior the subject of low wagers in gentlemen's clubs," he said weightily, rising on his toes a little as he spoke.

"And what, precisely, is the nature of the wager, John?" she asked crisply.

"It is not fit for your ears," he replied shortly.

"Nonsense, John! Don't be such an old woman!"

"It grieves me, Vivian, that you cannot have the ladylike manners of your cousin. If you were only more like Eustacia—"

"If I were only more like Eustacia, I could sneak about writing secret letters and carrying tales filled with half-truths! Don't be such a sapskull, John!"

John was silent for a moment while he struggled to control his temper. His sister had always been a thorn in his side, never regarding him with the respect he knew to be his due. She had loved their father and she loved Drake, she was even passionately fond of that worthless will o' the wisp, Tom Cane—but she could never keep a civil tongue in her head when speaking with him. Finally he gave way to his anger.

"If you must know, miss, they are wagering that Winter will leave you flat before a week has gone by."

"How could he, as you so neatly phrase it, 'leave me flat,' when there is nothing between us?"

"He has singled you out for particular attention, has he not?"

"He has danced with me, and he has come to call, and he has sent me roses. May I point out that I have danced with a good many gentlemen, and that some of them have come to call, and some of them have even sent me bouquets? Why are there no wagers about them?" she replied coldly.

"Because Winter, as you very well know, has a devilish reputation!" he shouted, pounding his fist into the palm of his other hand. As normally happened, she grew colder and baited him, while he gave way to temper. It goaded him to fury to realize that this chit of a girl could control her temper when he could not. "And you could not trouble yourself to think of your reputation or of our name before encouraging him!"

"It seems to me, John, that the problem is with the gentlemen who are making the wagers. If they are truly gentlemen, why would they bring the name of a lady into such a matter? And why do you choose to frequent places where such things are done?"

Stung by the element of truth in what she said, John raised his voice again and changed his tactics. "You have no consideration for anyone but yourself, Vivian! It does not matter to you that perhaps *I* might wish to marry and that the lady of my choice might not care to ally herself with a family that becomes the subject of such loose talk!"

For once his diversionary tactics worked perfectly. Vivian

froze, staring at him. "I did not know that you were engaged, John," she said slowly, trying to take that in and realize what it would mean to her and to her mother. "Who is the lady?"

John had the grace to look uncomfortable. "Well, I have not yet proposed to her. That is . . ."

She watched him curiously while he struggled for words. "I have not actually decided upon the lady as yet," he finally said in a low voice.

Vivian stared at him in disbelief and then began to laugh. "And I am supposed to be grieved for a lady whose identity you don't know—who certainly is feeling no distress in this matter because she has no idea that she is involved in it?" she asked, her sides shaking and tears beginning to stream down her cheeks. "How very like you, John!"

Her brother was too angry to have command of himself. It was happening as it always did—he felt and looked ridiculous, and she had behaved in a most unbecoming, unladylike, un*sisterly* manner.

He straightened his shoulders, gazed at her in what he considered to be a cool and reproving manner, and moved quietly to the door, abandoning his study to the enemy. He would have been more satisfied had he been able to see his sister a few minutes later. She wiped her eyes and grew calm, considering carefully what he had said, and the full import of it came home to her. After all these years, John clearly intended to marry. Once he did, his wife would be mistress of Trevelyan, of his Scottish estate, of this townhouse. There would be no place of their own for Mrs. Reddington or for her. She knew that John was far too tightfisted to think of setting them up in a small house of their own. They would be at the beck and call of him and his wife—and of the children that would doubtless follow quickly. She had seen that happen in other cases—grandmothers and maiden aunts who had dwindled into little better than servants in their own homes.

She sat quietly in the study, considering her situation. She did not have many choices. She could marry—if someone asked for her hand—and she could hope that he would be generous and provide a place for her mother, too. Or she could begin to sell her stories and hope that her writing would provide enough of an income to take care of them. She would have to apply herself to writing another story, however, for she could not bring herself to take *The Spy* to a publisher.

It was discouraging to think of all the time she had spent on her novel and to know that she could not use it. She had been delighted with it at first, simply because she had finished it. As that first glow of accomplishment had begun to fade, however, she had grown uneasy. Lord Lucifer was no longer merely a character in her tale—he had become Lord Winter. What had seemed a story of romance and adventure now seemed to have become little better than a libelous attack upon someone that she knew—and liked. Despite the fact she had made Lord Lucifer a spy, she could not bring herself to believe it of Lord Winter—a smuggler, yes, but not a spy. She had a sudden vision of what his expression would be after reading her manuscript and she could not bear the thought. *The Spy* would never be published.

Sighing, she left the study and climbed the stairs to her chamber to dress for the evening. She would be attending a dinner party and the theatre, and the night stretched before her like a vast expanse of desert she must cross. It would have been so much easier to face the ordeal if Lord Winter were to be a part of it.

She had told him no less than the truth when she had said she would miss him.

Chapter Eight

She set to work on a new story that very night, this time using Lady Connaught as a model and planning a story of intrigue and romance about that dashing lady. She worked until dawn that night and for the two nights that followed. Each time she grew weary, she pictured John and his wife and a horde of miniature versions of John. That acted as an adequate spur to keep her awake.

As she worked, she occasionally thought of Lord Winter and wondered where his business affairs had taken him. Could he possibly have returned to the Devon coast? She knew him to be a smuggler, or at least to have an investment in the smuggling trade—she had no doubt of that—but she could not bring herself to believe that he was a spy. That required a duplicity that she did not think him capable of.

"You nodcock," she told herself. "What do you really know of him to be able to judge *what* he is capable of?" This she knew to be the voice of reason, but she found that she could not accept it. She thought of Drake and the thousands of soldiers and sailors like him. Winter would surely not do something that would endanger their well-being. What could his gain be in such treachery? He would not be guilty of such a betrayal. He might be a cold man, but he was a man of honor.

"And how do you really know that?" she heard herself asking. "What are they to him? He seems to care for nobody, so what is to prevent his doing such a thing?" And the memory of the rumor that he had killed his own brother for gain kept returning, ignore it though she might.

The matter of Lady Connaught had begun to trouble her as well. The more she thought of it, the less she understood why she and Lord Winter were still separated when there appeared to be no bar to their relationship. And if the lady were truly his lost love, why had he been so attentive to a young lady from the provinces, attentive enough to attract the attention of most of the ton?

Amusing himself, no doubt, Vivian told herself, trying to redirect her attention to her writing. And yet—although he had clearly found her amusing—he had seemed sincerely drawn to her. And that, she reminded herself, was the hallmark of the most dangerous kind of flirt: the ability to make a girl believe that she was special. She was grateful when her weariness became so great that she could no longer remain awake, prey to her own wandering thoughts and voices.

When the maid awakened her by drawing the curtains, she awoke with a jerk. Groaning, she looked into her dressing table mirror. It was well that she was not subject to vanity, for dark shadows lay under her eyes and her small face looked almost pinched. When Tom came to call a few minutes later, she appropriated him immediately and, with no apology to anyone in the drawing room save her mother, for John had already left for his club, forced her friend to take her on a brisk walk.

"I must have something to revive me," she told him as they set out.

"I can see that you are scarcely in good skin," he said honestly, surveying her. "Has John upset you so much then?"

She shook her head. "Not John so much as what he plans to do."

"Which is what?" Tom inquired.

"He plans to marry," she replied briefly.

Tom stopped cold and stared at her. "No!" he exclaimed. "Stepping into parson's mousetrap after all these years? I thought that John planned to live his whole life as a comfortable, cranky old bachelor."

"So did I," she replied honestly. "but he now plans to be a cranky old family man. It was a dreadful blow to hear him say that and to know that Mama and I would be living at Trevelyan with John and his wife and their myriad children."

Tom shuddered at the thought. "Lord, yes. Bad enough to be with that stick-in-the-mud John. Terrible to add a passel of brats—particularly John's brats."

For a few minutes they walked on, enjoying a companionable dislike of John. It came to an abrupt halt, however, when Lord Winter pulled up alongside them in his curricle, holding his spirited team firmly in hand.

"Good-day, Miss Reddington, Mr. Cane," he said briskly, tipping his hat to her and nodding to Tom. "I trust that I find you in good health, ma'am. You don't look quite yourself today." He looked at her with some concern, and Tom, noticing it, took umbrage that he felt on intimate enough terms he could allude to Vivian's appearance.

"We are very well, thank you, sir," he responded stiffly, taking Vivian firmly by the elbow and guiding her along the street.

Lord Winter kept pace with them, however. "Are you certain, ma'am, that you are feeling quite the thing?" he asked Vivian, his concern clear.

"Yes, thank you, Lord Winter," she replied, smiling up at

him. In truth, the fresh air and exercise were helping—as was seeing him.

"Perhaps a quick turn around the Park would pick you up," he suggested.

Tom's eyes flashed. "That would not be necessary, sir," he replied firmly, "nor suitable. We will be turning back toward home in just a moment, at any rate."

Vivian, however, perhaps thinking of John, slipped from Tom's grasp and held up her gloved hand to Lord Winter who, though taken by surprise, handed her quickly into the curricle.

"Here now, Viv!" exclaimed young Mr. Cane, outraged. "You can't go riding with him—not without a chaperone."

"Forgive me, Tom," she replied penitently. "I am sorry to abandon you like this, but a brief drive may be just the thing. I shall only be a minute, and Lord Winter will return me to you directly."

"And I suppose that I'm to stand here cooling my heels while you trot off and make a cake of yourself?" he demanded indignantly. "Viv, you do beat the Dutch. I'll not do it."

"Then Lord Winter will drop me off at home, Tom, and I'll see you there."

"You most certainly shall!" he exclaimed. "You are the most tiresome chit I have ever known. It will be a wonder if John lets you live when he hears of this!"

"I fear that we have distressed Mr. Cane," commented Lord Winter smoothly as the curricle bowled on down the street.

"He will be quite all right," returned Vivian comfortably. "He never stays in a temper for very long."

"Does he not?" Lord Winter asked, glancing at her curiously. "And do you put him to the test very often?"

Vivian laughed. "I'm afraid that I do. Poor Tom! That was very shabby of me to leave him there."

Lord Winter nodded. "I am afraid that I must agree with you—although I am, naturally, very glad to have your company.

What have you been doing in my absence to tire yourself so much? Too many balls?''

She looked at him speculatively, wondering if she should mention Lady Connaught. "I have been keeping late nights with my scribbling," she replied, smiling.

"Indeed?" he asked, surprised that she was truly so serious about her writing. "And have you made any progress? Have you anything ready to send to a publisher, as you hoped?"

"I have made some progress. I had to lay aside the manuscript I had almost completed and start a new one, however."

"I am sorry to hear it. Did you not care for the old one?"

She shrugged. "Not as much as I once did." She glanced up at him. "What of you? Was your trip a satisfactory one?"

He shook his head. "It was not what I had hoped, I am afraid—but no matter." And he turned the subject lightly aside, adding, "Who have you met during the days I have been away? Anyone of interest?"

Feeling that she could not pass by such an opening, Vivian nodded and plunged in. "I met a most fascinating and beautiful woman, a Lady Connaught."

From the corner of her eye she saw him suddenly stiffen. "You will be best served, Miss Reddington," he informed her shortly, "if you have no dealings with Lady Connaught."

She turned to stare at him in disbelief, for he had always been casually playful in his tone toward her, never admonitory. She had not thought that he would become one more person to order her about.

"And why should I attend to what you have to say, sir?" she demanded, bristling. "Are you my father or my brother, to order me about so?"

Recognizing his lack of wisdom, he looked at her ruefully. "No. I am not your father, though I am quite old enough to be. Forgive me for being such a churl?" he asked, his dark eyes alight as he reached over and took her hand.

Disarmed by his apology and feeling suddenly self-conscious again, she nodded and took her hand away. "Why should I not speak with Lady Connaught?" she asked.

He paused, unable to tell her the truth, but she saw the pain in his eyes and said hurriedly, "Forgive me, Lord Winter. I should have realized that it would be difficult for you to be reminded of her. Forgive me for causing you pain."

He stared down at her for a moment, thinking of Lady Connaught. The contrast between the two women could not have been greater.

"Forgive me for being presumptuous," he said sincerely. "I know, Miss Reddington, how greatly you mislike being told what to do. I forgot myself."

Vivian, no longer bristling, sighed. "Everyone else does, Lord Winter. You may as well do so, too. Even Lacey and Tom instruct me in the best way to go on."

He smiled. "I shall not advise you about that, Miss Reddington. No one has ever accused me of knowing the proper way to go about things."

He was pleased to see her chuckle at this sally. "Perhaps I *should* take a page from your book, Lord Winter. No one dares to question you, whereas *everyone* would call me to order."

"Not if you were engaged to me," responded Lord Winter casually, wondering for a moment if he were a fool to be doing this. Still, it was such a small matter to him to make life more bearable for her, and it had been a very long time since he had wanted to do anything for anyone else.

"It need not be truly an engagement," he hastened to add, seeing her expression. "I am aware that you have no wish to marry—nor do I—but if people thought you were engaged to me, they would be much less likely to tell you what to do. If you would like the freedom to see some of London—and perhaps to put what you learn into your stories—this would be an effective way to do it. It would at least buy you time for your writing, with no one troubling you about what you *should* do. You could go your way and I could go mine.''

Vivian gasped. "Dare we do such a thing?" A sudden vision of Lacey's face—and John's—rose before her. Even life in London could be bearable under certain circumstances. It would be worth a great deal simply to be able to see Lacey's expression upon hearing of the engagement, after bearing all of Lacey's barbed comments about her lack of conquests. As for John— well, it would be worth any amount of money to see him confront Lord Winter. He would not have the strength of character to say no to him or to his money.

Lord Winter bowed. "With your permission, Miss Reddington, I shall wait upon your mother immediately and then I shall purchase your engagement ring."

At the mention of a ring, Vivian looked doubtful. "But a ring, Lord Winter—that seems so, so permanent. I would not keep it, of course," she hastened to add.

He smiled. "I should be desolated if you did not, Miss Reddington. And I shall enjoy our little adventure. It will give my life a measure of interest it has not had for some years now."

Comforted by the thought that she was doing something for him, Vivian allowed herself to be persuaded.

"But you will be speaking to John instead of my mother, Lord Winter," she told him. "He arrived in London just after you left and he was—" She broke off, trying to think of a tactful way to phrase it.

Lord Winter, who had heard of the wagering in the clubs, understood her perfectly. "He was—put out?" he inquired mildly.

Grateful, Vivian nodded. "John has a temper and he thinks very highly of himself," she explained.

"He does not sound a very taking sort of person," remarked her companion, "although the same could be said of me."

"He is a most odiously self-satisfied person, Lord Winter, and that you most certainly are not," replied Vivian firmly, determined not to allow him to compare himself to John.

He bowed to her, chuckling. "I see that I have a champion, Miss Reddington. I thank you—and I look forward to setting the odious John in his place for you."

Vivian smiled at the thought of it. John would never be able to hold his own against the man beside her. The only thing that she regretted was that their interview would be private and she would be denied the pleasure of seeing John bested.

When they arrived, the irate Mr. Cane was waiting upon the steps, and John, who had learned of his sister's perfidy, was watching from the drawing room window on the first floor, his mother and Lacey at his side.

Tom held up his hand to help her down, but Lord Winter sprang down, handing Tom the ribbons and taking charge of Vivian himself.

"My apologies, Mr. Cane, for leaving you standing on the street without your charming companion and for leaving you in charge of my team now."

"Leaving me in charge of your team?" exclaimed Tom in astonishment. "Most certainly not—"

"Allow me, because you have been so generous and because I understand that you are Miss Reddington's good friend, to give you our news and to ask you to be the first to wish us happy," inserted Lord Winter smoothly, bowing to Tom.

Tom's eyebrows arched almost to his hairline. "To wish you happy?" he exclaimed. "Do I understand you to be saying that—"

"Just so," nodded Winter with a friendly nod. "We have not yet chosen a date nor gotten a license, and I must ask permission of Mr. John Reddington, but we have quite made up our minds."

"Made up your minds?" repeated Tom blankly, staring from one to the other.

"Tom, can you say nothing except to repeat what is told to you?" demanded Vivian. "Will you not wish us happy?"

"Wish you happy?" repeated poor Tom again, trying to regain his balance in a world that was spinning dizzily. "You are really going to marry him, Viv?"

She nodded firmly. "Indeed I am, and I am in need of your support, Tom."

Thus called upon, Tom straightened his shoulders and tried to hold the world a little more firmly in place. "Then of course you have it, Viv, but—I have always stood your friend, even when you were—"

Thinking better of what he was about to say, he hurriedly added, "Of course I wish you happy." And he gave Vivian a brotherly peck on the cheek and shook Lord Winter's hand with a credible degree of firmness.

Lord Winter looked from Vivian to Tom. The engagement would be worth his time and effort just for its entertainment value. He looked forward to receiving congratulations from Mr. Roger Wilding as well. Then he glanced toward the drawing room window at those gathered there, particularly noting the arrogantly disapproving expression of one who must be Mr. John Reddington. He quite looked forward to meeting the gentleman. Life was looking much more interesting than it had earlier in the day.

"Shall we go in?" he inquired of Vivian, offering his arm. And together they went in to face the dragon.

Chapter Nine

The "dragon" seemed to grow perceptibly smaller and less fearsome when he viewed Lord Winter standing in the doorway of the drawing room.

"May I have the favor of a word with you in private, Mr. Reddington?" Lord Winter inquired gently, gazing down from his dark height upon John, who was accustomed to thinking of himself as a fine, strapping man. There was something very off-putting about an extremely tall gentleman with a scar that spoke of past experience in swordsmanship. John grew noticeably smaller—his sister almost felt it in her heart to pity him—as he led the way to his study.

She was left to share her news with her mother and Lacey. Mrs. Reddington, having allowed herself only to dream of such a thing, embraced her warmly, for she gave no credence to any of the things the ton whispered of Lord Winter, and his admiration of her daughter only served to confirm her opinion of his good sense. Lacey was scarlet with mortification that Vivian had received an offer from such a wealthy man when none of her admirers had, as Tom had coarsely expressed it earlier, "come up to scratch."

The outcome of the interview with John was precisely what she had known it would be. The two emerged from the study, her brother a little startled in expression but very prepared to wish her well.

"You will not believe," he whispered to her, "the settlement that he is prepared to make upon you, nor what you will have in the way of pin money, nor what he has promised to do for our family. My dear girl, this is beyond anything that I had imagined for you!"

Vivian was taken aback, for she had not anticipated this, and she glanced at her suitor, wide-eyed. He anticipated her, and smiled and nodded, fully prepared to make good upon his promises. "For, my dear Miss Reddington," he whispered to her later as he was saying good-bye, "just think what you have done for my self-esteem. I now have a family and I am looked up to as a provider of largesse. I have almost become respectable. Do not deny me my small pleasures."

She looked at him, a little puzzled, but she recognized his sincerity, and smiled.

"Thank you, Lord Winter," she whispered softly, standing on tiptoe to kiss him on the cheek. "You do me too much kindness."

He was to think of that later that evening. It had been a very long time since anyone had thanked him for any kindness—indeed, since he had done any kindness—and he had been taken unawares by the pleasure that it had given him. Vivian Reddington was very far from being a great beauty, and she was not what he had considered his ideal woman—if indeed there was such a thing—but she was very warm and very real and very loving. He stared into his glass that evening and shook a warning finger. "You will go too far in this little charade, you know," he said to his reflection, who nodded in agreement, "and then what will happen to you? What will Miss Reddington think of you when all is said and done?"

There was no answer, of course, for he lived a solitary existence. If he did not answer himself, or if his valet or one of his train of servants did not answer him, then there was indeed no answer. He had lived his life too long alone.

He presented himself promptly at Miss Reddington's home the next day, fully prepared to leap through whatever hoops the family thought fit to hold for him, and he was startled to see that he was received with open arms.

"Thank you, Lord Winter," whispered Mrs. Reddington. "She is the dearest of children—although difficult, of course— and I wish you very happy."

Somewhat bemused, he patted his mama-in-law-to-be on the hand and smiled. Vivian was watching him from across the drawing room, her smile somewhat painful.

"Do you think we should really be doing this, sir?" she murmured when he drew near to her and kissed her hand.

"Of course, ma'am," he assured her firmly, taking her fingers to his lips. "How could you think otherwise?"

And, leaning close to her, he whispered, "Just think of John, my dear girl, just think of John and a bevy of his children— and smile!"

Thus urged, Vivian smiled widely. And she continued to smile for what seemed to be weeks and spent endless hours engaged in polite conversation with virtual strangers.

She had not been prepared for the reaction to the announcement of her engagement to Lord Winter. When it was known abroad—and it was immediately, for John paid a call both to White's and to the newspaper—she had immediately suffered an onslaught of callers, cards, and bouquets. She had no idea that she had made so many acquaintances—she could call few of them friends—during her time in London. Her mother had spent hours with her, explaining what she was to expect and how she was to behave.

In short, she was exhausted. She longed for Trevelyan. She longed for Drake. On the fourth day of her engagement, having received what had become her customary stream of callers and well-wishers, she whispered to her mother, "I must go to my room, Mama. Indeed I must. Who *are* these people and what am I to say to them?"

Recognizing a plea for help, Mrs. Reddington called in Lord Winter, and they laid their plans. Vivian was to be exposed to no more gratuitous callers, no more people that she did not know who were seeking to congratulate her and ingratiate themselves.

"She is, after all, a writer, ma'am," observed Lord Winter to Mrs. Reddington. She regarded him blankly, for no one in the family took Vivian's scribbling seriously, but she said nothing.

"She needs some time for herself," he added firmly, fully alive to the obligations of their engagement. He was to enable her to write.

And, accordingly, Vivian was allowed her own time. While Lacey and Mrs. Reddington were receiving callers in the drawing room, Vivian was busily scribbling in her room above, protected from any recriminations by the very generous sum that Lord Winter had settled upon her. It was John himself who instructed the servants to leave her in peace while she was at work. And Vivian, mystified but happy, wrote steadily.

Now and then she went out socially, but always on the arm of her intended. It could scarcely have been more pleasant for her. She was not required to make small talk, nor to smile at strangers; she simply went out occasionally with Lord Winter and smiled—and that seemed to be all that was required of her. Apart from that, and from her private meetings with him, she continued to write, and no one troubled her or asked what she was doing. She could scarcely have been happier.

One thought kept troubling her, however. She still worried about Lord Winter's smuggling connections, and she wondered whether or not she should tell him that she had seen him before their first meeting at the ball. At first she could not have imagined confiding such a thing to him, but his unfailing kindness to her had eliminated almost all fear. The only thing she now feared was telling him about *The Spy*. He had asked if he might read something that she had written and that was the only completed manuscript she had with her in London. She had managed to avoid the problem, but her conscience continued to trouble her.

"You needn't show me anything if you don't wish to," he had assured her one afternoon as they were riding in the park.

"But I do wish to," she protested, turning to look at him earnestly. "No one else has ever taken my scribbling seriously, and if it weren't for you, I would have been allowed no time for it at all while we are here in London. As soon as I complete the piece that I am working on, I shall give it to you directly."

Lord Winter studied her thoughtfully. "I thought you had almost finished a book when you first arrived. It must be taking you longer than you had expected."

"Yes, it has been dreadful to finish," Vivian agreed unblushingly, seizing upon this straw. She would show him the new manuscript. She would need to change a few things so that Lady Connaught would not be identifiable at all, but the character in her new story had changed so much from the original model that she felt there was little chance of his recognizing his lost love.

She had encountered Lady Connaught several times since their engagement had been announced, and each time that lady had sought her out and made some allusion to her past engagement to Lord Winter.

"I am relieved that he has finally found someone that he feels comfortable with," she said patronizingly, gazing down at Vivian one afternoon at a card party. "He has been so long alone and grieving that I had feared he would never find another."

Vivian, fully alive to the fact that she had none of the real rights of a fiancée, nonetheless felt a burning desire to put that lady in her place. Everything that Lady Connaught said was fully intended to remind Vivian of the fact that she was the love of Lord Winter's life.

"He threatened to kill himself, to kill me, when I left him," she said sadly, having cornered Vivian one more time. "I feared for his life and his sanity for many years, but now—" She gazed down at Vivian and smiled beatifically. "Now he will have a little wife who will devote herself to him."

Vivian was burning to ask why Lord Winter had not asked Lady Connaught to devote herself to him, but remembering in time the nature of their engagement, forbore. After all, she reminded herself sharply, he might very well be in love with Lady Connaught still. What did she really know of Lord Winter?

She was thinking precisely that one evening when she was dancing with him at a ball. He still danced only with her, standing and watching while she danced with others.

She had not realized that she was studying his face until he said in amusement, "And what do you find there, Miss Reddington?"

"A gentleman who has done me a great kindness," she replied without hesitation. That much at least was emphatically true.

He bowed briefly, acknowledging her tribute. "I am honored to be allowed to do you a service, ma'am," he assured her.

There was a brief pause while he studied her, Vivian looking away at the other dancers to avoid looking into his eyes. "I wonder what else you see," he said slowly. "I sometimes feel that you see more than I would like for you to, my dear, for I am far from perfect."

"No one is perfect, Lord Winter," she said softly. "Why should you feel that you should be?"

He laughed. "I am so very far from perfect, and so many people would testify to that fact, that I don't know why I ever have a thought about perfection."

Vivian was not pleased by his levity and his quick dismissal of his own worth. "You treat yourself too lightly, my lord," she said seriously. "You must remember the worthy things you have done."

"And what would those be?" he asked in amusement.

"You have helped me and my family," she returned, "and, if I asked you, I am quite certain that you would help others."

"Perhaps," he said, "but only if you asked me. I do not go looking for charitable endeavors. In the meantime, it is enough for me if I have helped you and given you an opportunity to make a life for yourself. You have given me pleasure, my dear, and I should like to return the favor."

A minute or two later the dance had ended and he had led her into the shadowy garden. "Do you remember our first stroll in a garden?" he asked teasingly.

She smiled. "Of course, Lord Winter. I believe we should be looking for Tom and Mr. Wilding now."

He chuckled. "I wouldn't put it past them. They are probably lurking on the terrace now, preparing to sweep down and rescue you from danger."

Stopping suddenly, he pulled her close to him, crushing her cheek against his chest until she was aware of every fiber of material in his jacket—and even more aware of how natural it felt to be held in his arms like this, his lips upon her hair. She did not even murmur when he sank down upon a stone bench in a tiny arbor, gathering her onto his lap and pressing kisses on her neck and shoulders until she could scarcely catch her breath.

"Forgive me, Vivian," he said thickly, his kisses moving

from her throat to her eyelids to her lips. Finally he managed to stop and to move an inch or two away from her lips. ''I had forgotten—''

''Forgotten that we are engaged, sir?'' she asked, her eyes bright as she lifted her lips to his again.

''Never that, my dear,'' he murmured. ''Never that.''

Locked in the security of his arms, forgetting Lady Connaught and his wicked reputation, Vivian believed him. This was not Lord Lucifer, but her own dear love. He could no more be a spy and a murderer than could she herself.

''I wish that we were not pretending to be engaged,'' she whispered, gently tracing the scar on his cheek with her fingertip.

His grip upon her tightened painfully and he looked at her searchingly. ''Have you grown tired of it, my dear? Do you wish to cry off?''

Shaking her head violently, Vivian buried her face in his cravat, doing serious damage to its immaculate arrangement. Ignoring the havoc that she had wreaked, Lord Winter gently cupped her face in his hands and forced her to look into his eyes.

''Then why do you wish we were not pretending, Vivian?''

She attempted to bury her face once more, but he would not allow her to escape.

''May we give up this charade, Vivian?'' he asked, taking pity upon her. ''Would you, in truth, do me the honor of becoming my wife?''

Vivian lifted her face, smiling at him, and to his amazement, he felt his heart skip a beat. He had not thought that he would ever again feel so alive.

Just as he lowered his lips to hers, there was a sudden upheaval close by them as someone tripped over a pot of flowers and almost joined Vivian on his lap.

''Here now, Viv, Lord Winter! You're causing a scandal by

being out here so long!'' Tom said sharply, trying to right himself and retain a few shreds of dignity.

"Here they are, Wilding!'' he whispered into the darkness. "I've found them!''

In a matter of moments Lord Winter and Vivian found themselves cornered by her two guardian angels. The couple allowed themselves to be shepherded back toward the terrace, but when the light fell upon them, Mr. Wilding bleated in dismay.

"Your cravat!'' he said despairingly, looking at the ruins of Lord Winter's shirtfront. "You can't go into the ball like that.'' And drawing Lord Winter to one side, he proceeded to repair the damage as well as he could.

"Honestly, Viv, what a scapegrace you are!'' exclaimed Tom in a low voice. "Can't you ever behave properly?''

"But we are engaged, Tom! Aren't you happy for us? We are to be married!''

Mr. Wilding and Tom both stared at her blankly.

"Well, of course you're going to be married, you nodcock,'' replied Tom. "But that don't mean that you can run about acting like this. You've been missing from the ballroom long enough to set all of the old tabbies talking. Until you are safely married, Wilding and I are going to do our best to keep you out of trouble.''

Thinking of Drake, Mr. Wilding nodded emphatically, and together they shepherded their charges back into the ballroom.

Oblivious to the stares and knowing glances, Vivian danced happily through the remainder of the evening and rode home in a happy glow. No longer was she thinking only of her writing, nor could she picture a future that did not hold Lord Winter.

The one thing she must force herself to do now was to tell him about seeing him at Ben's, and about Lord Lucifer. She was quite determined to do it, and before she went to bed that evening, she searched her room for her manuscript of *The Spy*.

She had noticed earlier that she had misplaced it, but she

assumed that in the midst of the confusion of her engagement she had simply mislaid it and had not troubled herself unduly. It never occurred to her that Lacey might have picked it up and made it her own.

Unfortunately, that was precisely what had happened. Lacey, remembering the pages she had read in Vivian's room, had removed them from her lap desk and recopied them neatly, including all of the pages that had been marked through. Then she had cleverly written her own ending, leaving Lord Lucifer responsible not only for his own brother's death and assorted other acts of wickedness, but for the imminent threat of a French invasion. In her final scene, a series of hilltop bonfires to alert the countryside—like those planned in case of invasion a number of years ago, before Nelson had destroyed the French fleet— were set ablaze to notify the people that Boney and his men were about to land. Then, heavily veiled, she had taken the book to a well-known publisher.

"Everyone will recognize the people involved in this story," she told that gentleman. "You have only to publicize it, and the members of the ton will snap it up."

She was successful, for the publisher, scenting scandal, took her advice, publishing *The Spy* as a novel penned by A Young Lady of Society.

Vivian had continued to search for her manuscript the next morning. Lord Winter had sent another huge bouquet of "turkey-blood" roses and a note that he would call that afternoon.

A little later in the morning she went out to run some errands, intending to purchase a gift for him. Passing a shop with a display of books in the window, she saw one with a red leather cover and the title *The Spy* in gold letters across it. Coming to an abrupt halt, she caught her breath. Surely, she thought, someone else merely had the same title.

But she was, of course, quite wrong. No one else had. It was indeed her book, from start to finish, including all of the parts that she had taken out, along with a few additions. Horrified, she carried the volume home and sat with it in the privacy of her chamber, reading until late into the night. The afternoon and evening slipped by with no word from Lord Winter. He had undoubtedly seen the book, or heard of it, and must be angry beyond the telling.

How could such a thing have happened, she asked herself. How would it have gotten from her room to a publisher?

It was then that the truth began a dawn upon her, and she hurried down the passage to her cousin's room. "Lacey," she whispered, shaking that lady's shoulder in the dark of the night, "Lacey, did you do this? Were you responsible for publishing my novel?"

Sleepily, Eustacia confessed to her misdeed. "But there's no harm done, after all," she yawned, pulling the covers over her head. "After all, you wrote it, Vivian."

"But I didn't publish it, Lacey," she had whispered, shaking her cousin again as she attempted to return to sleep. "You know I didn't publish it. And I had crossed out most of the parts that you included."

"Oh, that!" Lacey shrugged and rolled over. "It took no effort to recopy those sections. They were the best of the lot, Viv. Why did you take them out?" she asked, turning over again and wrapping herself securely in the covers.

"Because they weren't true!" whispered Vivian desperately. "Can you hear me, Lacey? Because they weren't true! I wrote those things before I knew Lord Winter!"

"That's unfortunate," murmured Lacey. "Truly unfortunate. Are you certain?"

"Of course I'm certain!" exclaimed Vivian. "What's wrong with you, Lacey? Can you not determine what is true and what is false?"

"Of course I can!" returned Lacey sharply. "But can you? Are you really looking at your fiancé, Vivian? I believe you saw him more clearly earlier."

The silence was deep between them as Vivian stared down at her cousin. It really made no difference what she said, after all. She had written much of what Lacey had published—and everyone would know that Lord Winter was the man being described.

"What will he think of me?" she cried, pressing her hands to her cheeks. "What have I done to him?"

The only answer was a malicious chuckle from her cousin. "I can't see what the problem is, Vivian. After all, this is a work of fiction, is it not? Why would anyone take it as the truth? And, after all, I did you a favor. I got something of yours actually published—and Lord Winter, after all, has been encouraging your writing. He should be pleased."

Vivian stared down at her blindly, then rose and walked back to her own chamber. She could not berate Lacey. The responsibility was hers. She had written the book and had failed to keep it properly secured. She would have to tell Lord Winter what she had done—but she could not bear to think of what his expression would be when he discovered how she had betrayed him.

Chapter Ten

The ton was abuzz with news of *The Spy* by the next day. People rushed out to purchase it, and the delighted publisher, who had brought out the first printing in record time because he had suspected it would be just such a success, hurried to prepare another. There was no telling how long the fickle public would be calling for it, and he intended to make every last farthing possible while interest was high.

Vivian felt that she was caught in a nightmare. Leaving her solitary chamber because she could not bear to be alone, she sat in the drawing room that morning receiving streams of interested callers, curious to see how she was taking the news of the book. Lord Winter did not put in an appearance, however, so she was spared having to confess her part in all of it for the moment.

Predictably, her mother felt that there could be no truth in the story *The Spy* and that certainly it could have nothing at all to do with Lord Winter. John, who had just heard about it, felt that it *could* be true, but he did not wish it to be so. After all, he had agreed that his sister would be allied with the man, and he felt that his own honor would be compromised if Winter were really the one being written about. Too, Winter represented a substantial amount of wealth added to that of the Reddington family. He was determined that he would not allow it to be true, and denied any connection of Winter to the novel loudly and often.

Tom, who suspected the truth of the matter immediately, insisted upon a private audience with her.

"Have you read the thing, Viv?" he demanded when they were alone in John's small account room. "Do you know what it says about Winter?"

She nodded silently, the shadows dark under her eyes.

"You didn't—Tell me you didn't write this, Viv," he pleaded.

When she didn't reply or return his gaze, he clapped his hands to his forehead and collapsed into the nearest chair. "How *could* you do something so cork-brained, Viv? This isn't even scandalous—it's so far beyond scandalous that—" Here he broke off again and looked at her, wild-eyed.

"Has Winter seen this yet?" he demanded.

She gave a small, dismal shrug. "He didn't call yesterday, although he had promised to, and he hasn't yet called upon me today, so I haven't spoken with him yet."

A gleam of hope shone in Tom's eyes. "Perhaps there's a chance then. If he hasn't seen it, perhaps we—"

"Perhaps we can what?" asked Vivian hopelessly. "Buy all the other copies? Keep other people who have read it from talking to him? Tie him up and keep him in the cellar until everyone forgets about it?"

Tom slumped back down into his chair.

"Daresay that wouldn't work," observed Mr. Wilding, who had opened the door a little and was now looking round it carefully, as though inspecting the premises for Winter's presence. "I daresay we would have to keep him down there for years, and sooner or later someone would ask after him. Bound to."

He paused a moment to consider. "Nasty damp places, cellars. Dashed unhealthy—better think of another place," he recommended.

Vivian and Tom, who had thought themselves alone, turned toward the door.

"Did you overhear what we were talking about?" demanded Tom.

Mr. Wilding nodded. "Suspected as much myself," he said proudly. "After all, I know that you are a scribbler, Miss Reddington, and everyone knows that Winter is Lord Lucifer—already heard it at the club this morning."

Vivian groaned and fell among into the sofa cushions.

"I just asked your mother where I might find you—told her that I had something important to impart," said Mr. Wilding to her confidingly.

"Well, what can possibly be more important than this disaster?" demanded Tom, pointing at the copy of *The Spy*.

Wilding shook his head. "Don't know that it's *more* important," he replied doubtfully, "but the thing is, you see, I've had word from Drake."

Vivian turned toward him, her eyes bright. "Is Drake coming home on leave?" she asked hopefully. "Perhaps he could help me out of this scrape if he is."

"Don't know that he's on leave, exactly," demurred Mr. Wilding, "and I don't see that anyone could help with this deuce of a mess, but—"

"Wilding, you cawker, would you get to what you have to say?" demanded Tom. "I've never known of a fellow to take so long to make his point."

Mr. Wilding looked affronted, and drew himself up to his

full height. "I say, Cane, not a cawker—a Pink of the Ton, yes, but never a cawker. Why—"

Before he could embark upon an explanation of why he was not a cawker, Vivian put her hand on his sleeve and looked up at him pleadingly. "You know that Tom is just upset, Mr. Wilding, or he would never have said such a thing. Everyone knows that you are awake upon every suit, and I am so very grateful that Drake asked you to look after me."

Mr. Wilding looked gratified at this tribute, and glanced at Tom to see if the import of her words was having an effect. Unfortunately, Mr. Cane was grinning widely. "Coming it much too strong, Viv," he reproved her. "I'd give over pitching us another one of your Banbury tales when one of them has already gotten you into the suds."

"Never mind him," said Vivian comfortingly to Mr. Wilding. "He's always been a trifle maggoty."

"Rats in his upper works," agreed Mr. Wilding shortly, deciding to ignore Mr. Cane as one beyond human help. "Well, the thing is, you see—" He paused and looked at Tom again. "Need to speak with you privately, ma'am," he said in a low voice.

"Here now," protested Tom. "What sort of havey-cavey business is this, Wilding? I've known Viv all her life, and I'll not have you sending me about my business. If it involves Viv, it involves me."

"It's all right, Mr. Wilding," Vivian assured him. "Tom would never betray a confidence."

Mr. Wilding looked somewhat dubious, doubtful perhaps that one so afflicted could have full control of his mental faculties, but he continued after a moment. "Drake sent me a note," he said in a low voice, after making sure the door was firmly closed. "I am to travel down to Lynhurst—"

"To Lynhurst?" exclaimed Vivian.

He nodded. "Don't know just why," he replied. "Too early

to be staying along the coast there on a repairing lease. Told me to stay at The Golden Boar and wait until he got in touch with me." He shook his head. "Very peculiar, I thought. Not at all like Drake."

He looked at her and shook his head again. "Something very smoky about the whole business," he said slowly, "but I'm to go down tomorrow. And I wasn't to tell anyone about it, but I thought, in view of the circumstances, I'd best—"

Vivian pressed his hand gratefully. "Thank you, Mr. Wilding. I *do* need to see Drake. Perhaps he can tell me what to do."

"Well, if you hadn't written that book and published it, Viv, you wouldn't be in the basket now!" said Tom, returning to his earlier grievance. "Whatever made you do such a maggoty thing?"

"I didn't," Vivian replied flatly. Seeing his expression of disbelief, she hastened to add, "Oh, I wrote it all right—most of it at any rate—but I wrote it before I met Lord Winter."

"Before you met him!" exclaimed Tom incredulously. "How could you have described him in such detail if you hadn't yet met him?"

She had forgotten for the moment that the others knew nothing of her activities at Trevelyan, nothing of Ben and The Lighthouse. "I had heard stories about him, you see," she temporized. "And I just refined them a bit and put in some bits of my own."

"And then, like a nodcock, you published it, thinking no one would recognize him as the subject or you as the writer—when Winter himself knows all about your scribbling and encourages you in it." Tom stared at her, his eyebrows arched in disbelief. Even Mr. Wilding looked uncertain.

"Lacey published it," replied Vivian shortly. "She took it from my desk and sold it."

"That little vixen!" exclaimed Tom. "I knew she was a

sneaksby and a tattle-monger, but I'm dashed if I ever thought she'd do something like this!''

Vivian nodded dismally, her troubles washing back over her again. ''I couldn't believe it either, but she admitted it—and she doesn't care a button about the trouble she's caused.''

The three of them were silent for a moment, reflecting upon the perfidy of Miss Lavenham—although it could be suspected that Mr. Wilding's mind wandered, for he was seen to inspect a shadow on the snowy linen of his cravat, fearful that a spot had blemished its pristine brightness.

''I shall have to tell Lord Winter, of course,'' said Vivian, breaking the silence with a determined straightening of her shoulders. ''And then I am going down to Trevelyan, and after Mr. Wilding sees Drake, I shall expect Drake to come and see me at home.''

Mr. Wilding proved evasive on this point. ''Don't know that he'll do it, ma'am. I was supposed to keep mum about this, and I don't know what he's got on his mind. This could be a rum business.''

Vivian dismissed this objection with a wave of her hand. ''Drake wouldn't be involved in anything underhanded. And he'll see me if he knows I'm in trouble.''

She turned toward the door. ''If you'll forgive me, gentlemen, I must tell my mother that I need to go to Trevelyan immediately. She will understand that I need to get away from London for a few days.''

Tom began to look more hopeful. ''That could be the very thing to do, Viv,'' he agreed. ''What more natural than that you need a rest when you discover your fiancé written up in a book like this! Chances are no one except Winter will suspect that you wrote it, and you won't have to face him for a few days yet if you leave town. Perhaps by the time you come back we'll have thought of a way out of this scrape.''

Vivian shook her head. ''I have to see Lord Winter first and tell him the truth," she said firmly. "He deserves that much from me."

The butler appeared at her side, bearing a note on a silver salver. Vivian's heart sank as she looked down at it the bold, black ink on the heavy paper. It was from Lord Winter.

She unfolded it carefully, preparing herself for what it would say. The others watched her closely, waiting for a reaction. When she had finished it, she refolded it carefully and held it, still staring down at her lap.

"Well?" demanded Tom. "Was it from Winter, Viv? What does he have to say?"

Vivian nodded. "He congratulated me on the success of my first novel," she said in a small voice. "And he said that he was glad that he had been of some small service to me. He doesn't say a word about Lord Lucifer."

They waited, but she said nothing else for a few moments, still looking down at her hands and the note in her lap. Slowly she started to twist the handsome, square-set emerald that he had given her as an engagement ring.

"And he says that he is going away for a while, and I might find it easier to go out in public if I made it known that our engagement was at an end. He feels that I might find it embarrassing to be the fiancée of someone that many will now consider a traitor to king and country."

Tom and Mr. Wilding shifted uncomfortably at the sight of her brimming eyes.

"No use to flood us now, Viv," said Tom hastily, searching for his handkerchief. "It wasn't really your fault after all."

She shook her head sharply . "You know that isn't the truth, Tom. It was entirely my fault! And now he's had to go away because of it."

"That doesn't sound much like Winter," returned Tom thoughtfully. "He hasn't ever given twopence for what anyone else thought about him. Why would he take this so much to heart?''

"Has some people stirred up," observed Mr. Wilding. "At the club this morning, they were wagering on how long it will be before Winter is brought up on charges.''

"Charges!" Vivian exclaimed. "What kind of charges, Mr. Wilding?''

Mr. Wilding, who never liked to be the bearer of bad news, shifted uncomfortably, wishing he hadn't mentioned it. "Serious ones, I'm afraid," he said slowly. "Sounds unlikely, I know, but it's what they are saying.''

"What are they saying?" asked Tom. "What are the charges?''

"Treason," he responded.

"Treason!" Vivian exclaimed, shocked, and even Tom looked taken aback. "How could they bring charges of treason against him? What does that have to do with my book?''

Mr. Wilding began to look desperate, but he plunged ahead. "Seems that there was rumors about before all this, Miss Reddington, but your book makes them believe that where there's smoke, there's fire.''

Vivian covered her face with her hands. She had known that the publication of her book was a harmful thing, bound to stir up more cruel gossip about Lord Winter, but she had never thought that it could have such damning consequences.

Tom, seeing her reaction, patted her on the shoulder. "Now, Viv, don't get into a pelter. Chances are that it's all talk. Winter has always been the focus for gossip and rumor—this will all die down and just become a part of the things whispered about him. No one will take it seriously.''

Grateful for any ray of hope, Vivian took down her hands and looked at him. "Do you really think so, Tom? Not but what it is a terrible thing to have stirred up more gossip about him—but I couldn't bear to think that I had brought something so terrible as a charge of treason upon him.''

''You may be sure that it will die down,'' said Tom firmly, sounding much more confident than he felt.

Mr. Wilding, however, had been shaking his head slowly. ''Don't know that you're right there, Cane,'' he said dubiously. ''Seems to me that some of those I heard at the club this morning meant business. Said that for a peer of the realm to be guilty of fratricide was one thing, but to be guilty of opening the door for Bonaparte—well, that was quite another.''

Tom looked at him in exasperation, as Vivian lapsed back into her tearful state, accepting Mr. Wilding's handkerchief gratefully. ''At least Winter is out of town,'' he said. ''Perhaps we can think of a way to handle this situation while we're down at Trevelyan.''

Vivian and Mr. Wilding looked at him in surprise. ''Don't think for a minute that I'm going to let you go down there by yourself, Viv. There's no telling what outrageous notion you might take into your head. You need someone sensible along with you.''

Although she could not believe that they could think of a way out of the bramble bush she was in, Vivian was more than willing to go to Trevelyan and hope for the best. Drake would be close by and he had always been able to take charge of things; surely he would have an idea that would be helpful. They had to think of some way to help Lord Winter. She had tried to imagine what his expression had been when he learned of her betrayal, and she discovered that she was able to picture it all too well.

The piercing happiness she had felt for the first time only two days ago was replaced now with a pain that was almost as sharp. Not only had she lost Lord Winter's love, but she had also held him up for public ridicule and accusation. She could never return things to the way they had been between them, but at least she would do what she could to help him.

And she wondered just where Lord Winter's business affairs might have taken him this time. She wanted to find out from Ben if he had returned to The Lighthouse since the last time she had seen him there.

Chapter Eleven

Vivian, accompanied by Mrs. Reddington, Lacey, and Tom, returned to Trevelyan for a brief stay the very next day. Tom, of course, was to stay at his own home, but he rode down with them and planned to spend most of each day with them. Lacey had no desire to leave London, and she complained frequently and loudly about the inconvenience of the journey and the boredom that would overtake her at Trevelyan and the balls that she would be missing in London. Vivian, naturally, was unmoved by her complaints, and even Mrs. Reddington—although unaware of Lacey's role in their present troubles—was unconcerned, pointing out that Vivian's needs must take precedence in the current situation. That did nothing to comfort Eustacia, and her complaints continued until Mrs. Reddington forbade her to say another word about their journey.

They had not been home for more than half an hour before Vivian had changed and gone down to the stable to saddle Pimm. There she had a quiet word with Joe, who told her that things had gone from bad to worse during her absence.

"It's that Hawkins, Miss," he told her grimly. "Two more men wounded after old Ben, and the body of Jim Cutler, a free trader from down the coast, washed ashore just yesterday. Shot through the heart, he was."

"Has the law done nothing about it?" she asked anxiously, worried about Ben's welfare.

Joe gave a brief snort. "Waring? He went over to Grassmere, and Hawkins told him he was that sorry to hear of such violence in our neighborhood. Told Waring he was fair worrit about his family, bein' out in such a lonesome spot. Asked Waring for protection."

"Can't the free traders band together?" Vivian asked. "Then he wouldn't dare to come against so many of them."

"They can't agree among themselves who should be in charge. Every man jack of them thinks he should be the one, so they can't get ahead in making any plans."

"Then it's time they did," Vivian announced briskly, swinging up into the saddle and saluting Joe with her riding crop as she prepared to leave. "Just between you and me, Joe, I'm going to The Lighthouse to see Ben, but don't tell Mr. Cane if he comes looking for me."

"To The Lighthouse?" gasped Joe, horrified. "But you can't, Miss, you must stay clear of that place."

Vivian waved back at him. "I'll take my chances, Joe," she called, moving Pimm quickly into action. "I'll be back before dinner."

She followed her old path along the top of the cliff, taking comfort in the water pounding the rocks below her, the short, sharp cry of the sea-mews, and the quiet peace of the familiar scene. Somehow her troubles in London seemed very far away now—and somehow more manageable. She picked her way carefully down the narrow path and into her old hiding place, securing Pimm and then slipping into the secret cellar.

A moment's check after lighting her candle revealed that her bundle of clothing was still in its place in the keg, and she changed hurriedly, tucking her curls under her cap. She slipped quietly into place in the darkened chimney corner of the taproom and let her eyes adjust to the lighting. There were few people there today, for the day was fair and the wind brisk. There were one or two locals that she recognized and one man that she couldn't recall having seen before seated at a table not too far from her, but she gave no sign of studying them or anyone else in the room. Instead she sat and nursed the tankard of ale she had poured for herself as she came in, keeping her gaze down.

After a while a snatch of conversation reached her. The men were talking of Hawkins.

"A bitter black shame it is!" exclaimed one of them sharply.

"Aye," nodded one of his companions. "Jim Cutler was a fine, honest man. He shouldn't have met his end like that. There's never been bloodshed along this part of the coast— the trade's been an honest business, safe enough to have your sons work it, too."

There was a murmur of agreement and again she heard the name of Hawkins mentioned.

It was then that the door opened and Ben entered, accompanied by two other men. One she saw illuminated by the bright sunlight and she recognized immediately—it was James Hawkins! The other men in the taproom grew silent at the sight of him. The third man—and here her heart sank—the third man was Lord Winter. She had no need to see his face to know him. She recognized his form, his walk, and then she heard the low murmur of his voice. Instantly she shrank farther into the shadows, hoping to conceal her presence.

"Well, Marley, what say you?" she heard Lord Winter say. "Does Hawkins's offer sound reasonable to you or not?"

Ben shook his head. "It does not, sir. I'd be giving him too much and I'd not have enough left to make a living on. It's little enough I take in as it is.''

Lord Winter laughed shortly. ''My heart goes out to you, landlord, but I beg to differ. I believe you make a very good living indeed, and I think you will continue to do so if you join forces with Hawkins.''

''That's easy enough for you to say,'' returned Ben staunchly, ''but I'm the one that'll have to live with it, and I say it's too much.''

''It appears we are at point nonplus, Hawkins,'' commented Lord Winter casually. ''What is your suggestion?''

''I think Marley knows what my suggestion is,'' remarked Hawkins casually, leaning against the wall and slowly tamping down tobacco in his pipe and lighting it. ''How's your shoulder these days, landlord?''

Vivian's hands tightened around her tankard as she listened to this blatant reference to Ben's wound. Just a reminder of what could happen again—and of the fact that this time it need not be a shot just to wound. How could Winter be working with a man like Hawkins?

There was no answer and inadvertently she glanced up. Ben was staring directly at her, but his eyes dropped as soon as they met hers. Lord Winter, who had followed this bit of byplay, glanced sharply toward the hearth corner, and Vivian ducked her head and nursed her tankard.

''It appears your nephew is here today,'' commented Lord Winter, indicating Vivian.

Ben nodded. ''So he is. I reckon his ship made port sooner than he'd thought.''

And he nodded briefly in Vivian's direction. She nodded back, giving her cap a brief tug of acknowledgement and lowering her eyes. So Ben had put about the story he had promised. She smiled grimly to herself. At least he hadn't killed her off yet so that she was a visitor from beyond the grave.

She grew more serious immediately, however, because the men moved in the direction of the hearth, still talking.

"I'd hate to see trouble here, Marley," said Hawkins casually, cleaning the mud off of his boots on one of the well-scrubbed andirons Ben took pride in. His place might be rather a poor one, he had told Vivian when she was younger, but he kept it as spotless as some kept their fine posting houses.

Ben said nothing, either in reply or about the careless treatment of his andirons.

"Perhaps it can be avoided," observed Lord Winter, and Vivian felt her heart begin to beat faster at his proximity. She could almost have reached out and touched him. "Surely two men of good sense can work something out."

Hawkins spread his palms out helplessly. "You see, sir, that I have done what I can," he responded. "It shan't be on my conscience if anything goes amiss."

"Conscience!" exclaimed Ben bitterly. "What does a man like you know of conscience, Hawkins?"

Hawkins turned toward Lord Winter and shook his head. "Do you see what I'm up against?" he inquired. "There is no reasoning with any of them."

"Why should we reason with those who wish to rob us? With those who set upon us and kill us?" demanded Ben.

Gently, Ben, gently, Vivian found herself thinking. *Don't provoke this man to do something desperate.* She was absolutely certain that Ben was right and that Hawkins had no conscience. He would not be troubled by simply killing Ben instead of wounding him.

And what did that say about Lord Winter? she asked herself. How did he fit into all of this? She would have loved to ask him, but of course she could not without endangering Ben— and perhaps herself. She thought unhappily of her book. Perhaps it had been more accurate than even she had thought.

It was a bitter discovery, and she could take no pleasure in it. She had come to love Lord Winter, yet it appeared that he was every inch the rake she had painted him originally in *The Spy*. Not actually a spy, perhaps, she corrected herself—not that, surely—but at least knee-deep in smuggling and connected with a scoundrel like James Hawkins.

She had almost grown angry as she sat there, mulling all of it over and gripping her tankard more and more tightly, but then she remembered the backhand turn she had served him by publishing the book. Even though it had been Lacey's doing, she would have had nothing to work with without Vivian's help. Sighing, she sank farther into her corner.

Her sigh was apparently louder than she had thought, for she heard Lord Winter say, "Is there a problem, boy? That was a gusty sigh for one so young."

Before she could move, Ben had moved swiftly between them, effectively blocking her from their view.

"He's always been a boy that felt things overmuch," he said in explanation, speaking over his shoulder to them. "His ma's been poorly lately, and he's afeared that she's not much longer for this world." And bending over Vivian, he patted her comfortingly on the shoulder and whispered, "At the first chance, get out of here, m'dear."

Turning back to the others, he stood directly in front of her, affording her all the protection of his considerable breadth and the old-fashioned flared skirts of his jacket. She huddled there, eyes down, until the front door again opened and again a man was silhouetted against the bright sunlight of the late afternoon.

Everyone in the taproom glanced up, and it took only a moment for Vivian to identify the newcomer. It was Drake. He had a moustache and beard and his hat was pulled low over his eyes, but she would have known him anywhere.

She sat there frozen while the three in front of her moved toward him and the men at the table watched. This, she knew, was her chance. She had to leave before she took the chance of Drake recognizing her. Silently she slipped into the passage-way and moved quickly down to the second cellar, changed, and untethered Pimm.

Before she could mount him, however, her arm was taken in a firm grip. She did not scream, although she took in her breath sharply and reached for her riding crop with her free hand. She was not allowed to reach it, however, and both her wrists were firmly grasped as she was pulled round to face her captor.

"Lord Winter!" she exclaimed.

He made her a brief, ironic bow. "Miss Reddington." Keeping his grip firm, he looked down at her, his expression cold. She thought that she had never seen his eyes look so distant and icy, certainly not with her. Winter seemed a very fitting name for him.

"I had not thought to have the pleasure of seeing you so soon, ma'am, let alone in such company."

"If you were a gentleman, you'd not be holding me captive, sir!" she said sharply, struggling to be free.

"Ah, but you've touched upon the heart of it there, my dear. As your book points out so clearly, I am very far from being a gentleman. Of course, I might mention that a lady would probably not be masquerading as the nephew of a smuggler at an inn where ruffians gather."

The mention of her book brought back in a flood the guilt she felt for the wrong she had done him. Now, however, she reminded herself sharply, it appeared that her early assessment of his character had been the correct one.

"For any injustices that I have done you in my book, Lord Winter, I apologize deeply." She had decided that she would not mention that Lacey had been responsible for its publication. That would have a ring of childishness she could not bring herself to be guilty of. Ultimately the responsibility was her own.

"Very clever, Miss Reddington," he said approvingly. "You do not commit yourself to any belief in my innocence—you merely say in a backhand way that you believe you have caught my character fairly, and if you have missed in any small detail, you apologize for your lack of accuracy."

She flushed hotly. "There was a time—a very short time ago, sir—when I was certain that my novel was wrong and my Lord Lucifer was a world apart from you. I was prepared to beg your forgiveness most humbly."

"Indeed?" he asked, a ring of surprise in his voice, although he did not loosen his grip upon her wrists. "And what has happened to change your mind?"

"You have," she returned sharply. "I find you here with James Hawkins, an outlaw who kills honest people and threatens them, as he does my friend Ben Marley, while you allow it to happen and show yourself to be on his side."

"Your friend Ben Marley is a smuggler, Miss Reddington," he reminded her, then caught himself. "But of course you know that, since you have been masquerading as his 'nevvy.' "

"Ben is a smuggler, but he's an honest free tradesman like most of the men along this part of the coast. There was never trouble until Hawkins came along a few years ago—and you came soon afterwards."

"Was it you who took care of him when he was shot this spring? I heard it was his nephew that saved him."

"Yes, I did it and he survived it nicely—no thanks to your Mr. Hawkins and his greedy, violent ways."

Lord Winter's grip on her wrists tightened unbearably and she cried out in pain. "Don't you realize, you little fool, that you could get killed doing what you did that night—or for that matter coming here this afternoon? Haven't you a grain of good sense or caution?"

She didn't answer, and devoted her concentration to biting her lip and holding back the tears of pain.

"No? I might have known." He released her suddenly, so that she almost tumbled over from the shock of it. "Get yourself home, Miss Reddington, and stay clear of this place or you'll find yourself hurt."

"Threatening me, Lord Winter?" she inquired bitterly. "I had thought that I had wronged you terribly in my book, and I wept over it and would have told you of it and apologized for what I had done—but I see that I simply didn't paint you blackguard enough."

"Very true, my dear," he agreed, pulling her close to him once more and kissing her firmly. "You did not put in everything. Perhaps I shall give you enough for a second volume."

Picking her up as though she were no more than a feather, he slung her on Pimm's back, placed the reins in her hands, and gave the pony a slap on the rump. "Stay home where you are safe, Miss Reddington," he advised her sharply.

All the way home her mind whirled. Lord Winter must indeed be as evil a man as she had at first pictured him, doubtless in league with Hawkins. Then she thought of the man she had known in London and she could not accept that. Unless he perhaps had two distinct personalities, she could think of no explanation for what was happening. How could the man she had grown so fond of—no, the man she *loved*—be hand in glove with a man like Hawkins?

And what on earth could Drake be doing with such men as these? Why was he so far from Wellington and his army? Why was he here secretly, without telling his family?

It was a long, long ride back to Trevelyan, and when she went to bed that night, it was not to sleep. The moon rose and set, and Vivian still lay awake.

Whatever was going on?

Chapter Twelve

The night brought no answers, nor did the morning. No one commented on her haggard appearance except Lacey, who noted tartly that if they had come to Trevelyan so that Vivian could rest, it appeared that she could do a better job of it. Otherwise, they might just as well return to London. Everyone else ignored her, however, and the subject was dropped.

It was not until the afternoon that Mr. Wilding joined them, and Vivian greeted him as one greets a long-lost friend from childhood. Naturally enough, neither Mrs. Reddington nor Eustacia had been aware that he was to be in the neighborhood, so they were amazed to see him in such an out-of-the-way place.

"Just passing by," he explained. When they looked doubtful, he hurried to add, "Been over to the Golden Bear in Lynhurst. Felt that sea air might be just the thing for my constitution, you know."

Since Mr. Wilding looked exceedingly healthy and, were he not, there were spas by the sea far closer to London and far more appealing to the ton than Lynhurst, Mrs. Reddington and Lacey regarded him with even greater amazement.

Their astonishment increased when Vivian said quickly, "That was very wise of you. You cannot be too careful of your health, Mr. Wilding."

"Just what I thought," he responded, gratified that someone had seen the wisdom of his decision. "Had weak lungs since I was a child. Must take every opportunity to build them up."

"Indeed you must," agreed Vivian. "In fact, Mr. Wilding, allow me to suggest a stroll through our gardens so that you may take in the bracing sea air."

Mr. Wilding, who had just settled himself with a glass of port and a biscuit, looked a little taken aback by this offer of healthful recreation, but Tom too descended upon him, almost lifting him bodily from his chair.

"It would be just the thing, old fellow," Tom told him heartily, setting the glass of port on a piecrust table next to his chair. "When we come back in, the port will serve to revive you nicely."

Mr. Wilding, who was beginning to grasp their meaning, rose nobly to the occasion. "Just so," he agreed somewhat feebly, casting a longing gaze at the port. "A last stroll in the late afternoon should be the very thing."

"The very thing to give him an inflammation of the lungs and carry him away," observed Lacey as the door closed behind Mr. Wilding and his two companions. "Whatever is he doing here, Aunt?"

Mrs. Reddington, who was equally mystified, simply shook her head. "I daresay we shall never know," she said simply. "It appears to me that Mr. Wilding is a more difficult man to understand than I had at first thought him."

Lacey, who had strolled to the window and was holding back the drapery, watched the trio thoughtfully as they descended into the garden. "There is certainly something more here than meets the eye," she agreed slowly.

It took Vivian and Tom some time to make themselves privy to Mr. Wilding's information. It appeared that Drake had come to his chamber at the Golden Boar very late the night before, and had awakened Mr. Wilding from an exceedingly sound sleep, partially induced by several glasses of the excellent brandy the landlord had provided from his personal store.

"French," he said judicially. "Smuggled goods of course, not surprising in this part of the world. And excellent—a warmth, a body, a fragrance that—"

"Never mind the brandy, Wilding," Tom told him sharply. "What of Drake? What did he tell you?"

Mr. Wilding shook his head in puzzlement. "Very peculiar, he was. In fact, if it hadn't been Drake, I would have said the fellow was all about in his wits."

"Did he tell you, Mr. Wilding," asked Vivian very patiently, "why he is here?"

Mr. Wilding shook his head. "Told me he wasn't here just for the sake of bringing me brandy—though of course I *knew* that. Said he needed for me to do something for him."

Vivian and Tom exchanged glances. So Drake had come here with smugglers. That much was evident to them, if not to the somewhat befuddled Mr. Wilding.

"And what was that?" asked Vivian. "Did he want you to carry a message to someone?"

Again he shook his head. "Gave me a snuff box and told me to hold it for him. Said he would fetch it very soon and I was to keep it on my person."

"Are you to stay in Lynhurst, then?" asked Vivian.

Mr. Wilding nodded. "I stay two more nights and then I return to London. Drake said that if he doesn't collect the box from me here, I'm to keep it until he comes to London for it."

"Do you have it with you?" asked Tom curiously.

Again Mr. Wilding nodded, and he pulled a graceful silver box from a deep pocket in his jacket. On its cover was a delicate butterfly, elegantly picked out in gleaming jewels.

"A very fine piece," commented Mr. Wilding unnecessarily. "Haven't ever seen one quite like it—the butterfly, you know, quite sets it apart."

"It is lovely," Vivian agreed. "But I don't understand why it is so important to Drake."

"The very thing I said," nodded Mr. Wilding, pleased to find someone in agreement with him. " 'Why, you don't even take snuff,' I said to him."

"And what did he reply?" asked Tom.

"Said that wasn't the point, that the box was important for other reasons—didn't tell me what they were, though." Mr. Wilding looked somewhat aggrieved. "Could have at least told me that. Here I sit—stuck in this backwater during the height of the season—and for what, I ask you? For a snuff box."

Vivian ran her hand over its surface and then shook it lightly. "There's something in it!" she exclaimed, tilting it so that she could hear the sound of movement.

"Bound to be," agreed Wilding. "Snuff, of course."

"I don't think so," said Vivian, holding it to her ear. "It sounds different."

Mr. Wilding took it from her and slipped it back into his capacious pocket. "Best to keep it put away," he explained. "That's what Drake told me—asked me not to open it, too."

Vivian's face fell. "I see," she replied. "Well, I guess it's just as well. We might lose whatever there is that's of importance."

She stood for a moment looking out to sea, for the garden was on the seaward side of Trevelyan. "Did you ask him to come and see me?" she asked suddenly, turning to Mr. Wilding.

Mr. Wilding nodded uncomfortably. "Told him. Told him that you were in the briars and needed to talk to him."

"What did he say?" she inquired.

"Said he would come if he could," Mr. Wilding said slowly, clearly unhappy about being the bearer of such tidings. "Don't seem very gentlemanly nor brotherly, I know, but then he don't seem too much like Drake just now."

"Well, you've done all you can," she returned, hoping that her disappointment was not too apparent, "and I'm indebted to you, Mr. Wilding. It was very kind of you to speak to Drake for me, and to come this afternoon to tell me what had transpired."

"If he can help, he'll be here, my dear—never fear it," Mr. Wilding said slowly, sorry not to be able to bring her happier tidings.

"Yes, I'm sure he will," Vivian replied automatically. How very unlike Drake this was. Always vitally concerned about his little sister, he had given her freely of his time, again and again, whenever her problems arose. Now, however, there seemed to be little likelihood of his coming to see her at Trevelyan—now when she needed his advice and help more than she ever had in her life.

Puzzled, she prepared herself for bed very slowly that evening. It was not like Drake to avoid seeing her. He had always made her first in his affection and taken care of her needs very carefully. How did it all fit together? she wondered. Lord Winter, a charming, difficult, enigmatic man; Hawkins, treacherous and greedy; Ben, kindly and steady; and Drake, charming, adventurous, and courageous. How did they all belong together? She was almost afraid of finding the answer.

Vivian had thought to visit the beach below The Lighthouse that night, thinking that with all of them present, they might be landing a shipment. She had forgotten, however, that there was to be a full moon, and it lighted all of the countryside with a silvery radiance that stripped away any hope of concealment.

No self-respecting free trader would take himself out on such a night. The chances of capture were too great.

She stood a long while at her chamber window, staring out over the gardens that stretched toward the cliffs. When she opened the window to let in the cold night air, she could hear the roar of the stream that tumbled down the gorge to the waters of the Channel. Where was Drake? she wondered. With Lord Winter? If so, did Drake know that she had been betrothed to him? Did Lord Winter know Drake's true identity? Was Winter truly a spy, as well as a smuggler? Too many questions whirled about in her head, but the soothing sound of the water finally caused her to drift off to sleep, her head on the sill of the open window, wrapped in her bedcovers.

She was amazed to see Mr. Wilding appear very early the next morning, almost before they had finished breakfasting. Since that was not his habit, and since she was certain he had been comforting himself with the innkeeper's supply of French brandy, it had doubtlessly taken something of great significance to move him.

"Is there something amiss, Mr. Wilding?" she asked with real concern, for his face was flushed and he seemed short of breath.

"Only too much brandy, dear lady, and too much exertion in riding this long way so early in the morning," he assured her, sitting down abruptly on the sofa. "Allow me to give you a message from Drake."

Suddenly alert, she leaned forward in her chair, grateful that her mother and Lacey were still at the table. She heard the sounds of their approach, however, and hurriedly tucked the note that he handed her into her pocket.

"More," whispered Mr. Wilding conspiratorially, fishing from his capacious pocket the snuff box. "This too," and he dropped it into her hand. Her eyes grew wide, but she slipped it into her pocket with the note, anxious to be able to read Drake's message and to have an opportunity to question Mr. Wilding further.

Her opportunity did not come quickly, however, for Mrs. Reddington, determined to be hospitable in return for Mr. Wilding's kindness in London, persisted in chatting with him and plying him with refreshments. Tom arrived before the hour was out, but before he and Vivian could force Mr. Wilding out for another bracing walk in the sea air, a messenger came from The Golden Boar.

"Fear I must go," Mr. Wilding announced abruptly, after excusing himself a moment to read the note just handed to him.

"Not bad news, I hope," said Mrs. Reddington, concerned by her guest's sudden pallor.

"Most kind of you, ma'am," he replied automatically, bowing to the ladies in the room and shaking hands abruptly with Tom. "I shall hope for the same thing myself." And with little more ado, he bowed himself out of the room, leaving the others mystified.

"He grows stranger with every meeting," said Lacey, her eyes wide. "What could possibly have been so urgent as to have forced him to race away in such an ill-mannered fashion? Mr. Wilding may be odd, but he has always been courteous."

Mrs. Reddington too looked puzzled. "I do hope that everything is all right," she said slowly.

Tom and Vivian exchanged glances, but Vivian made no attempt to communicate to him the news that she had the snuff box now—and a note.

It was much later when she was able to be certain of being alone. Lacey showed no inclination to honor Vivian's privacy, appearing unannounced in her room with some degree of frequency. "Probably to see if I have another book in hand so that she may publish it, too, and cause me infinitely more grief,'' she had observed bitterly to Tom when telling him of her cousin's annoying new habit.

Accordingly, it was not until she had ridden out alone on Pimm that afternoon that she made certain of being uninterrupted. In a secluded glade fresh with the tender green of early May she unfolded her note carefully, smoothing it across her knees.

It was indeed from Drake, written in his dear, familiar scrawl. "Keep the snuff box safely hidden, Viv," he had written, "and forgive me for not seeing you myself, but I fear it would endanger you. I should not have asked poor Wilding to come, but I had no one else I could trust implicitly and who could move about freely without attracting suspicion. His wit may not be swift, but his heart has always been loyal, and I knew I could count upon him to come. I am sorry for your present trouble, but do not despair. We will work it out." And he had signed it with love—and, by the look of it, had written it hastily.

She read it again, committing it to memory, and then shredded it into pieces too fine ever to be pasted together again. Then she buried the fragments and placed a rock over them. Lacey had made her cautious. She was quite sure now that her cousin went through everything of hers, reading all that she could place her hands on.

Uneasily she thought through the note again. Why, she wondered, was Roger Wilding no longer to keep the snuff box? She patted her pocket to be certain it was securely in place— she could not leave it in her room with Lacey poking about so much. And how did Drake think they could work out her problem? Did he truly know what her problem was? The more she thought, the less certain she was of the meaning of anything. She would have liked beyond anything to ride to The Lighthouse, but she knew that such an act could bring disaster upon herself and others, so she turned Pimm inland and took her ride across the moors, seeing no one but an occasional countryman.

When she reached Trevelyan, Joe was waiting for her at the stable. "There be trouble of some kind up at the house, Miss," he told her grimly, helping her down from Pimm.

"What kind of trouble?" Vivian asked, alarmed. "Has someone been hurt?"

"I don't know the rights of it, Miss, but a rider came from Lynhurst, and Mr. Cane ran out of the house, flung himself upon his horse and careened off down the lane, riding as though all the devils in hell was after him."

"Thank you, Joe," she said hastily, handing him the reins and running toward the house.

Her mother was watching for her from the window, and came to the door quickly. "It is the most unfortunate thing!" she exclaimed. "Poor Mr. Wilding!"

"What has happened to Mr. Wilding?" Vivian asked, taking a deep breath to calm the racing of her heart. She had been certain that the news was about Drake.

"They found him at the bottom of a cliff not far from Lynhurst. His horse must have thrown him and the poor man went right over the edge!"

Vivian's knees gave way and she sat down abruptly. "Is he—is he dead, then?" she asked in a dazed voice.

"Very nearly, or at least that was his state when the messenger came from The Golden Boar. The landlord was quite beside himself, and he knew that Mr. Wilding had ridden out here to see friends, so he sent for one of us. Tom was here, and he has gone to see what is to be done."

Mrs. Reddington took out her handkerchief and dabbed at her eyes. "That poor man," she said compassionately. "I don't believe he has any family to speak of—at least none that he or Drake ever mentioned. I don't know who should be informed of this. Drake will be distraught when he hears of it."

Vivian knew that that was no more than the truth, and she felt with equal certainty that it was because of whatever Drake was involved in that Mr. Wilding lay dying at The Golden Boar. She was certain that James Hawkins was somehow responsible for the violence done against Mr. Wilding—it was typical of him—but she did not know what to think about Lord Winter. Until now she had felt guilt-ridden each time she had thought of Lord Winter and her betrayal of him. She found herself wondering now, however, just how he was involved in all of this, and whether or not he were in any way responsible for Mr. Wilding's "accident." And, worse than that, she wondered whether or not the same thing might befall Drake.

When Tom returned to Trevelyan that evening, his face made it clear that he was the bearer of bad tidings.

"Has poor Mr. Wilding died then?" cried Mrs. Reddington, holding her hands to her mouth. "What a terrible, terrible accident! I have always known the cliff path was treacherous! Vivian, I forbid you to ride upon it again!"

"Did he regain consciousness, Tom?" asked Vivian, saddened by the death of her friend.

Tom shook his head. "At least not according to the surgeon who attended him. I wasn't allowed to see him, of course."

"Do we need to make the arrangements for him?" asked Mrs. Reddington. "After all, he was a dear friend of Drake's."

Tom and Vivian exchanged glances. "There appears to be no need," replied Tom slowly. "By the time I got there this afternoon, the landlord had found a letter that Wilding had left on a table in his chambers before setting out to Trevelyan."

"What sort of letter?" asked Vivian, her brow wrinkling.

Tom shrugged. "The landlord didn't offer it to me to read, but he said that Wilding had left instructions about what to do should anything happen to him."

"How very strange," said Vivian slowly. "Why would Mr. Wilding do such a thing as that? He was a very young man with no reason to suspect his death might be imminent."

But he did have a reason, she said to herself. Drake's note

had indicated as much. She patted the snuffbox, still in her pocket. Someone—probably Hawkins and Lord Winter— wanted it very badly.

Tom appeared to be suspicious too, but he merely replied, "The landlord said that he hadn't found it when he sent the messenger out to Trevelyan this afternoon. At that point, he wasn't sure what he was supposed to be doing about Wilding."

"Why did the first messenger come for Mr. Wilding earlier?" Vivian asked, suddenly remembering the episode of the morning. "When he left us so suddenly to go back into Lynhurst, it was because of a message. Did the landlord tell you what it was?"

Tom looked suddenly blank. "I had forgotten completely about that," he responded. "That will bear looking into."

"What do you mean?" demanded Lacey sharply. "Why would it 'bear looking into?' What's going on here, Tom? Wasn't this an accident?"

"I don't know that anything is going on, Eustacia," he responded. "We're merely thinking aloud. People frequently do that when they're overwrought."

Lacey lapsed into silence, but she continued to watch them closely, and Vivian wasn't surprised to notice later that evening that Lacey had been searching her room again. Gently she tapped the snuff box in her pocket. It would stay with her.

Chapter Thirteen

It seemed very strange to Vivian to know that Drake was so near and yet she couldn't talk with him. He had been gone now for a year, but she had felt closer through their letters when he was in Spain than she felt now, when he was only a few miles away with no communication between them. Just what it would take for him to be able to come to see her seemed a mystery. Her mother, she knew, would faint dead away should he walk in unannounced. As for Lacey, Vivian knew that she would do her best to draw Drake's attention to herself and hold it there. She had been stalking him for almost two years now, though fortunately Drake showed no sign of interest.

As she sat at her window that night, saying a silent prayer for poor Mr. Wilding, she saw a slight movement in the shadowy garden below, and she leaned out farther to try to see more clearly. A pebble bounced lightly on the glass above her head.

"Viv?" The voice from below was very faint.

"Tom? Is that you?" she whispered as loudly as she dared. Her mother's chamber was on this side of the house, too, but fortunately it was next to Vivian's. Lacey's was across the passageway, so her windows looked out over the drive rather than the garden.

"Come to the door and let me in."

Hastily pulling on a dressing gown and transferring the snuff box to its capacious pocket, Vivian hurried as quietly as she could down the stairs, avoiding one creaky step she remembered at the bottom. Opening the door carefully, she peered into the darkness.

"Tom?" she whispered.

"Come out here and shut the door," he commanded in a low voice. "I need to talk to you."

Leading her down a path toward the cleave, he stopped at a point where the sound of the rushing stream kept their voices from being heard.

"I've been over to Lynhurst nosing around," he told her, bending close despite the fact that it would have been impossible for anyone to have overheard them. "I wanted to find out more about Wilding, and I thought about the snuff box."

Vivian started to speak, but he held up his hand. "Just let me finish, Viv. If you begin, I won't ever get a word in edgewise."

He waited a moment to be certain that she wasn't going to interrupt, then continued. "Viv, I don't think there's a body!"

She stared at him through the gloom. "What do you mean, Tom? What are you talking about?" she demanded.

"Wilding," he replied. "I asked where his body was being kept until it was shipped back to London, and I wanted to offer to pay for the coffin and make the arrangements, but the landlord said his body was still in his chamber and then he clammed right up."

"Well, you already knew that much, Tom. He had told you Mr. Wilding had left instructions."

Tom shook his head. "I found the maid that took care of

Wilding's chamber. She said that she had already cleaned the room and that Wilding had been taken away.''

''Did she say where he was taken? Was there a coffin already prepared?''

''She didn't know. But I asked her where his belongings were, his trunk and whatnot, and she didn't know that either. They weren't on the premises. But she *did* know where I could find the surgeon who took care of him.''

''Did you talk to him?''

''Naturally. He opened right up after a glass of brandy. After two or three, he became almost chatty.''

''Well?'' demanded Viv. ''What did you discover?''

''That he didn't see Wilding die. That he hasn't signed any death certificate.''

Vivian stared at him. ''Do you mean that you think Mr. Wilding is still alive?'' she asked slowly. ''But what would that mean? How could he still be alive if he went over the cliff?''

''I've done it, too, Viv. Remember? When we were kids?''

Vivian shook her head. ''Of course I remember that, Tom—but we *were* children and you fell onto a sandy part that only had a few rocks—and not from as great a height, either.''

She thought another moment. ''If he isn't dead, Tom, then why would they go to all the trouble of hiding him? What could he possibly have or know that they want—or want to keep hidden?''

''The snuff box,'' Tom replied confidently.

Vivian shook her head and reached into her pocket. ''I don't think so,'' she responded, and held up the silver box for him to see.

''He gave it to me this morning, along with a note from Drake,'' she explained. ''I haven't had an opportunity to tell you about them.''

She glanced up at his face when he remained silent. ''Well,

it's true, Tom,'' she snapped. "When could I possibly have told you today? Did you want to share the news with Lacey?''

He examined the box carefully. "I think that we may need to open it after all," he said thoughtfully. "Maybe it would help us.''

He stared at her for a moment longer, then asked, "What did Drake have to say?''

"He told me to keep the box safe, and that he was sorry he couldn't help me with my trouble. He held out a hope that we might be able to work something out later.''

"I think we should open the box," he said firmly.

"We must open it inside where we can see properly and be certain that we aren't losing something important from it," she replied, reclaiming the box.

Accordingly, they slipped quietly back into Trevelyan, closing the library door quietly behind them after lighting tapers in the room. Everything looked as it should—except that the two of them, wide-eyed and more than a little frightened, were staring at the snuff box on the table there as though it had had a hypnotic effect upon them.

Tom prized the box open carefully with his thumbnail, and they both bent over to look inside it. All that it contained was a simple twist of paper. Carefully they smoothed it out and held it closely to the light.

"What in blazes does it say?" demanded Tom, trying to hold it closer to the flame.

"You're going to set it afire, Tom!" hissed Vivian. She lay it flat on the library table once again and scrutinized it carefully.

"Of course we can't read it," she replied. "It's a cipher.''

Tom stared at her blankly a moment. "A cipher? Do you mean this is some sort of secret message? Like the ones we used to play at when I was in short coats?''

Vivian nodded briefly, trying to piece it all together. They sat silently for a moment.

"What would Drake be doing with something like this?" mused Tom. "It's as plain as a pikestaff that this is something that is important to him."

"With poor Mr. Wilding dead because of it, I believe we can safely say that," she agreed dryly. "Between that and the fact that Drake won't come near me, I should say that his business is *very* important."

"His business? Then Drake must be—" Tom began.

Vivian nodded again. "A spy," she said, completing his thought. "We should have guessed as much."

Tom looked indignant. "Well, that's a pretty thing to say! Why would we even suspect such a thing?"

"Because Drake is with Wellington's staff and Wellington is not, at the moment, in the Bristol Channel. Drake is."

"Don't take that tone of voice with me, Vivian Reddington!" he snapped. "You sound exactly like Crewett, pointing out where I had gone wrong in my lesson."

"Poor Crewett always had my sympathy," returned Vivian briskly, beginning to feel more herself as she studied the paper before her. "Being your tutor must have been the devil's own business. I don't see how he survived it or how he ever managed to teach you enough to get you in to Oxford."

Tom was fully prepared to do battle over this slur upon his academic record—accurate though it was—when the door of the library suddenly swung open.

"I thought as much!" said Lacey sharply, stepping into the room and holding her taper higher. "Vivian, have you lost every vestige of propriety? John will *not* be pleased to learn that you are entertaining gentlemen unchaperoned in the middle of the night—and in your dressing gown."

"Lacey, would you give over being such a paperskull?" asked Tom impatiently, rising and blocking Lacey's view of the table as he turned.

Vivian took advantage of this deft maneuver to slip the paper into her pocket. She was not quite quick enough, however.

"A love letter, Vivian?" she inquired coyly. "I would not have imagined that Thomas had so much imagination."

Tom looked repelled. "A love letter? Have you lost what little sense you ever had, Lacey? What would give you such a shatter-brained notion?"

"What else would bring you here in the middle of the night?" inquired Lacey, determined to discover the truth of the situation.

"Can't see that it's any of your affair," returned Tom curtly. "You're not Viv's mother."

"I can go and awaken Aunt if you like," said Lacey, smiling maliciously.

"Just do that little thing," he said. "She already thinks that you're the greatest tattle-box in Christendom after the way you went haring to John about her business. Why not show her that she was precisely right?"

Eustacia paused a moment. "I *am* going to tell her," she said stiffly, looking back at them from the doorway. "I feel that it is my duty to do so."

"Then go and do your duty, Lacey," said Viv in an exhausted voice. "Just stop talking about it and do it."

In high dudgeon, Lacey left the library and directed her steps toward Mrs. Reddington's chamber.

"What a dust she is kicking up over nothing at all," commented Tom in amazement. "I daresay she felt that I should offer for you immediately, never mind the fact that you're betrothed to Winter—or at least you were."

He considered this for a moment, then returned to musing over what they had been saying before they were interrupted, and his brows snapped together. "Viv, if we think that someone tried to kill Wilding to get the snuff box, and they discover he doesn't have it, what do we think they will do next?"

Vivian had already considered this. "They will retrace his

steps and try to determine where he might successfully have hidden it."

"Which means that at some point they will think of you," he said flatly.

"Or perhaps of you," she added. "You spoke with him, too."

They considered the implications of all this for a minute or two and then Vivian again broke the silence.

"You remember that Mr. Wilding brought me a note from Drake this morning as well as the snuff box," Vivian said quietly, "so Drake at least knows that he came here. It is not so likely that the others will know of it."

"Did Drake tell you he's a spy in that note? Is that how you came by the notion?"

"Of course not, Tom, you simpleton! Why would a spy set down that information on paper for all the world to see? We have already seen tonight how carefully they send their written messages."

Putting her hand into her pocket again, she drew out the tightly folded message from the snuff box, and Tom scrutinized it carefully.

"Well, I can't make hide nor hair of it," he said finally, rubbing his hand across his eyes.

"Of course you can't as yet," Vivian agreed. "We'll have to work out the key later. It may take us a bit, but we'll manage it."

A sound on the stairs caused Vivian to sweep the note safely out of sight once more.

"Thomas!" said Mrs. Reddington crossly as Lacey opened the door for her. "You are the most tiresome boy! I couldn't credit my ears at first when Lacey told me you were here. Whatever are you doing here in the middle of the night? Why can't you pay your calls like normal people?"

"It's obvious, Aunt—" began Lacey importantly, but Mrs. Reddington cut her short.

"It's nothing of the sort!" she said briefly to her niece. "Well, Thomas," she temporized, thinking of some of Tom's past escapades, "I don't know why I act so amazed at your out of the way behavior. I do recall your doing this when you and Vivian planned to run away to sea."

"Here, now, Mrs. Reddington, no need to dwell on the past," said Tom hurriedly.

"You came over here to tell Vivian that you had changed your mind and decided that life at sea might not be all you had thought it. The two of you woke up the entire household brangling down here when Vivian called you a coward and tried to force you to go."

She paused in her reminiscences for a moment and looked at her daughter sharply. "You're not thinking of doing anything so foolish again, are you?"

Vivian laughed, glad to have diverted her mother's thoughts to harmless matters. "What? Of running away to sea? I can assure you that you are perfectly safe, Mama. Tom is still fearful of life at sea—except for taking out his sailboat, of course."

"Here now, Viv!" cut in Tom, irritated at this slur upon his manhood. "Only a nodcock would take ship with some of the ruffians you see in port. I may not be a downy one, but I don't have rats in my upper works."

His annoyed glance at Vivian indicated the distinct possibility that she might suffer from such a disability.

"Thomas, it is too dark a night for you to be riding home," Mrs. Reddington informed him. "I will have Parker make up a chamber for you."

Turning to Lacey, she said, "Come along, Lacey. There is no need for you to have your night's rest disturbed any longer."

"But, Aunt, aren't you going to say something to Vivian

about her lack of conduct?'' demanded Lacey, unwilling to leave while there was any possibily of learning something more. ''And Tom hasn't explained what he is doing here tonight.''

''You needn't give it a thought,'' Mrs. Reddington told her briskly. ''Tom and Vivian have never needed a reason to behave outrageously, as you should know well after all these years. All we lack now is Drake coming in to laugh in the midst of all of this.''

Tom and Vivian glanced quickly at one another, a move that was not lost upon Lacey, although she could think of no satisfactory reason for it. Tom and Vivian were hustled off in different directions by Mrs. Reddington, and Tom soon found himself in a guest chamber, being helped out of his gear by one of the footmen, who had been awakened and hurriedly pressed into service as a valet.

Before going to bed herself, Vivian stood for a while longer at her chamber window, watching the garden below to be certain that Drake was not lingering anywhere in the vicinity. When her mother had made the remark about him, she had almost expected to look up and see him standing in the doorway, chuckling at their surprise.

Then, remembering Roger Wilding, she knew that there would have been no merriment. This was no childish lark, but a life-and-death business. Except, she reminded herself, that there was no body.

Chapter Fourteen

Tom appeared at what could only be termed an indecently early hour the next morning. As he had hoped, Vivian was the only one down for breakfast at that hour, and the two of them sat together and mused over the events of the past few days, trying to piece things together. Tom, of course, was missing a number of significant pieces, since he knew nothing of Ben and the smuggling, nor of Lord Winter's connections. She could not decide whether to take him entirely into her confidence or not.

"I have been thinking, Viv, that I had best move over here and stay at Trevelyan," he said seriously.

Vivian stared at him for a moment, her brows raised.

"Well, don't look at me like that! Just think about it for a moment. Wilding is dead—or if not dead, spirited away somewhere—and why? Because he had the snuff box—or because someone thought he had it."

He looked at her to see if she was following his line of

thinking carefully enough. "And who has it now?" he inquired patiently, trying to guide her.

"I do of course, you nodcock," she replied absently. "Don't ask idiotic questions."

"A dashed lot of good it does for me to try to help you, Viv!" he exclaimed indignantly. "All you can do is sit about and make insulting remarks and stare off out the window. Who knows what kind of people may be searching for that box? Or when they may decide to come looking for it here?"

"If it's Hawkins, we're in a lot of trouble, Tom," Vivian commented slowly. "He wouldn't hesitate to kill all of us if we gave him any trouble."

"Hawkins? James Hawkins?" asked Tom, beginning to feel distinctly uncomfortable. "Why do you think he might be the one, Viv? He operates a good distance from here."

"He has moved into our part of the world," she explained, still staring blankly out the window. It was so hard to know exactly what she should do.

"How would you know something like that, Viv? I never heard of it!"

"Servants," she responded briefly, still deep in thought.

"Some of your servants just happened to mention this to you casually?" he inquired caustically. "Just happened to stroll up to you and mention that Hawkins is doing his business in our neighborhood now, so we'd best all start carrying guns and guarding our women?"

"Well, perhaps the message really didn't amount to all of that," she conceded, laughing, "but I will say that Joe isn't normally frightened of anything, and he was clearly nervous when he was telling me about Hawkins. He had heard that Hawkins has already killed and wounded several honest men."

Tom grimaced. "Scarcely reassuring." He lapsed into deep thought, finally emerging to say, "I'm going to get my gear and bring it over here, Viv. Before I come back, though, I'm going to Lynhurst to see if I can pick up any news."

Vivian nodded. "I'm going to work on the cipher. It may be a simple one, easy to break. Drake used to read about such things and I know there are some things in Papa's library if I can only find them."

"Whatever you do, Viv, keep that snuff box with you and stay inside. Don't even take a stroll in the garden. We don't know what's going on, and I don't want anything happening to you."

Vivian frowned. "It can't be as bad as all that, Tom. Not yet. I'll be careful, though," she added hurriedly, seeing his darkening expression. There was no use in having a battle with him now.

Feeling that he had made his point, Tom departed, leaving her to take possession of the library in peace. The others wouldn't be down for a while, and Lacey almost never darkened the door of the library, declaring that she found so great a gathering of books in one place oppressive. Vivian smiled to herself. She would have loved the library anyway, but the fact that Lacey couldn't abide it was an added benefit.

A quick survey of the shelves on military history yielded a few volumes for her to look through, and she began patiently working her way through them. Julius Caesar had used a very simple substitution cipher, merely moving four letters down the alphabet so that A became D, and so on. She tried variations of that idea, but her attempts yielded no success. She had been working for over an hour when her mother and Lacey appeared in the doorway.

"Has Thomas gone home, dear?" asked Mrs. Reddington.

"Yes, Mama, but he will be back this afternoon. Tom has decided to take up residence with us for a while."

"How delightful," said Lacey caustically. "I don't recall his being invited to do so."

"Don't be foolish, Lacey," returned Mrs. Reddington, a little sharply. "Of course Thomas needs no formal invitation. This is his second home, and naturally since his family is in London, staying here is probably more sensible. Less trouble for the staff and more company for Thomas."

There was a slight pause as Mrs. Reddington looked steadily at Lacey, waiting for her to comment that John would disapprove of this arrangement. She opened her lips, but appeared to think better of it. Satisfied that she had made her point about who was in charge at Trevelyan at the present moment, Mrs. Reddington said to her, "Do go and tell Cook that there will be one more for dinner tonight, Lacey."

Reluctantly, Lacey departed. She felt that she was missing something important that was taking place, but she had not been able to discern just what it was. It had always been that way when Tom and Vivian or Vivian and Drake were together. They formed a unit in which she had no part.

"Working on your writing, dear?" inquired Mrs. Reddington cheerfully.

Vivian nodded, pleased that her working in the library was so much taken for granted that it would not attract any particular comment. Her mother closed the door behind her, saying that she would send some tea in to Vivian a little later in the morning.

A little more research turned up another cipher that depended upon a key word or phrase; this method had first been published in 1563, and a man named Vigenère had refined it a few years later, developing what was called the Vigenère Tableau. She studied the table for a few minutes, appreciating the cleverness of its simplicity. The table could be drawn up quickly from memory and the key word applied to the message to decipher it. She worked methodically, trying two or three common words like "England" and "Nelson" and "Trafalgar," but none of them yielded fruit. She had put the note back in her pocket and was staring at the table when she realized that she was no longer alone.

"How curious that is, Vivian. What are you doing? Learning your letters again?"

"Certainly," replied Vivian, closing the book and sweeping up the papers upon which she had been practicing. Lacey's question had not been too far off the target, for the Vigenère Tableau looked like practice with making one's letters:

A B C D E F G H I J K L M N O P Q R S T U V W X Y Z

A a b c d e f g h i j k l m n o p q r s t u v w x y z
B b c d e f g h i j k l m n o p q r s t u v w x y z a
C c d e f g h i j k l m n o p q r s t u v w x y z a b
D d e f g h i j k l m n o p q r s t u v w x y z a b c
E e f g h i j k l m n o p q r s t u v w x y z a b c d
F f g h i j k l m n o p q r s t u v w x y z a b c d e
G g h i j k l m n o p q r s t u v w x y z a b c d e f
H h i j k l m n o p q r s t u v w x y z a b c d e f g
I i j k l m n o p q r s t u v w x y z a b c d e f g h
J j k l m n o p q r s t u v w x y z a b c d e f g h i
K k l m n o p q r s t u v w x y z a b c d e f g h i j
L l m n o p q r s t u v w x y z a b c d e f g h i j k
M m n o p q r s t u v w x y z a b c d e f g h i j k l
N n o p q r s t u v w x y z a b c d e f g h i j k l m
O o p q r s t u v w x y z a b c d e f g h i j k l m n
P p q r s t u v w x y z a b c d e f g h i j k l m n o
Q q r s t u v w x y z a b c d e f g h i j k l m n o p
R r s t u v w x y z a b c d e f g h i j k l m n o p q
S s t u v w x y z a b c d e f g h i j k l m n o p q r
T t u v w x y z a b c d e f g h i j k l m n o p q r s
U u v w x y z a b c d e f g h i j k l m n o p q r s t
V v w x y z a b c d e f g h i j k l m n o p q r s t u
W w x y z a b c d e f g h i j k l m n o p q r s t u v
X x y z a b c d e f g h i j k l m n o p q r s t u v w

Y y z a b c d e f g h i j k l m n o p q r s t u v w x
Z z a b c d e f g h i j k l m n o p q r s t u v w x y

Lacey eyed her curiously. "What are you up to, Vivian?" she asked. "I know that you and Tom are involved in something odd. Does it have anything to do with Mr. Wilding's death?"

"Of course not!" snapped Vivian. "How would Tom and I have been connected to such a thing?" Trust Lacey to start nosing about at precisely the wrong time, she thought resentfully.

"I don't know," replied Lacey thoughtfully. "That is exactly what I have been wondering."

"Eustacia," said Vivian, trying to act as though her cousin were very far from the truth, "I believe that you had better take yourself back to London. Being in the country for too long appears to have affected your wits."

Lacey ignored this jab, and continued as though Vivian had said nothing at all. "Another thing that has been troubling me, Vivian, is just how you knew so many things about Lord Winter that were apparently true—and knew them before we arrived at London."

Caught entirely by surprise, Vivian could merely stare at her. Finally she managed to say coolly, "Precisely what do you mean by that, Lacey?"

"Just what I said. You had written a great deal of your book before we arrived in London. You didn't add all of the material about Lord Winter in just a few days." She studied Vivian's face closely. "So just how *did* you gain that knowledge, Vivian?"

"Lacey, you know that I was writing a fictional piece. It was a great surprise to me to learn that there really was a man who fit at least a little of the description I had created in my book. After I saw Lord Winter, of course, I added a few other details—but I had made him up out of whole cloth. That's why

I was so shocked to meet a man who appeared to be—in some ways at least—like the character in my book.''

Lacey was clearly unconvinced, but she smiled at Vivian and said slowly, ''Of course. It was all a matter of chance—with the greatest coincidence of all being your engagement to this same gentleman. How very, *very* peculiar.''

Vivian shut the library door behind her cousin and paced nervously up and down the room. What did Lacey have on her mind? She could not think of any immediate way that she could do them any harm, but it was always a mistake to underestimate Lacey. It was far better to try to anticipate any trouble she might cause them so that they could plan to minimize the damage.

Weary of pacing and of trying to work out the cipher, Vivian decided that she would take Pimm out for a ride. Not to The Lighthouse, of course, for she had promised Ben—but at least out to clear her head.

Joe saddled Pimm for her, shaking his head as he watched them gallop off into the distance. ''Stay clear of the cliffs, Miss,'' he had told her, reminding her of the accident. Nodding, she had started off with no intention of going near them, but the lure of them had drawn her inexorably. Riding across the moor and down lanes between hedgerows bright with flowers was enjoyable, but it did not bring the sense of freedom offered by the cliffs and the sea. She had stopped at the top of Lover's Leap, a high outcropping of rock with a sheer face that dropped straight to the sea. All that she could hear was the pounding of the waves against the rocks below, flinging up rainbows of spray, and the lonely, piercing cry of the sea-mews above. She left Pimm cropping some grass, his reins dragging free, and walked toward the edge where she could look out at the passing ships.

There was no warning—not a shadow, not a rustling, no sensation of someone else's presence. She felt a sudden thrust between her shoulder blades that sent her falling forward. The shock was almost too great for her to react, for she struck her forehead as she fell, but her instincts were strong and she grasped an outcropping of rock and hung on for dear life. She could feel someone trying to lift her, trying to pry her fingers loose so she could be shoved on over the edge of the cliff that was only inches away. She could feel the warm blood spilling down from her wound, and she had to close her eyes, but she did not relax her grip.

Suddenly she was aware that there was a third person with them. The one who had been pulling at her hands was jerked abruptly away and she could hear the sounds of a struggle. Turning her head, she tried to open her eyes and see what was taking place. She caught a glimpse of a figure she knew and her heart sank.

It was Lord Winter.

She blinked her eyes and tried to clear her vision so that she could see more clearly what was taking place and who the other man was, but the world began to spin and darkness closed in on her.

When Vivian regained consciousness, she was at Trevelyan in her own familiar bed, with her mother sitting anxiously by her side, dabbing at her face now and then with a cooling cloth.

"Are you all right, Vivian?" she asked anxiously as her daughter's eyelashes fluttered. "Tell me if you can hear me, my dear."

Having one of the stablehands running up to the house that afternoon to bring the news that Pimm had returned without his rider had been one of the most frightening experiences of her life. She had always feared for Vivian, although she had tried not to worry unduly so that she would not die young of an apoplectic attack, but she had been much more nervous since Mr. Wilding's terrible accident. That had been all she could think of when Parker brought her the news and informed her that Joe and one of the other stablehands had ridden out to search for her. Tom had returned at about the same time and had joined them, arriving back at Trevelyan an hour later, carrying Vivian crumpled in his arms. Joe had already ridden for the surgeon at Lynhurst.

When the surgeon and Vivian had both assured her that she had regained consciousness and truly had the use of all her faculties, Mrs. Reddington relaxed enough to retire to the kitchen to superintend the making of a beef tea to strengthen her daughter, leaving Tom at her bedside.

"You gudgeon, Viv!" he had whispered when the others had left. "I told you not to leave the house, now didn't I? What the devil possessed you?"

Disregarding his comments as frivolous, Vivian stared at him and said, "How did you find me, Tom? Where was I?"

Tom looked at her blankly. "Have you lost your memory, Viv? We found you just where the cliff path meets your property."

She shook her head. "That's not where it happened," she said. "It happened at Lover's Leap."

He moved restlessly. "See here, Viv. That's a mile away. You couldn't have come so far after you were hurt in your fall." He looked at her sharply. "And it wasn't like you to take a fall from Pimm. I can't remember that ever happening."

"It didn't," she said soberly. "I wasn't on Pimm when it happened."

"When what happened?"

"When someone tried to push me over the cliff. That's how I got this." And she touched the bandage on her forehead gingerly.

Tom sat down as though his knees had buckled under him.

"So it was just as we feared then," he said. "Someone *is* after the box. Did they get it, Viv?"

She shook her head. "I hid it before I went on my ride. It's safe for the moment."

"It may be, but I'm not so certain that you are," he replied. "Did you catch a glimpse of who did this to you, Viv?"

She turned her head to the wall. "I blacked out," she said. "I could hear them struggling, but that is the last that I recall."

"Well, someone saved you, my girl," he said frankly. "It would have taken nothing at all to have thrown you over the cliff after you were unconscious. Instead, someone carried you back almost to your own home and left you where you would doubtlessly have been found, if not by sundown, then at that time when the day servants started down that path toward the village."

Vivian thought long and hard that evening. She could remember two men struggling and she was certain that she had seen Lord Winter. The other man had not been distinct at all and her vision had blurred quickly after that and then dimmed.

Had it been Lord Winter that tried to kill her? Or had he been the one to rescue her?

She found that she could not accept the thought that he would deliberately do her harm. No matter what she thought of James Hawkins and Winter's involvement with him, she could not think so poorly of him as to believe him guilty of murder—particularly of her murder. She had not been able to believe he was connected with Mr. Wilding's death either, and so had not told Tom about his presence in the area or his connection with Hawkins.

The more she considered the matter, the more certain she was that Lord Winter had saved her, that he was trying to protect her. Drake was the only other person who would have fought for her, and she felt certain that she would have recognized him, even in her muddled state at the time of the attack.

Having concluded that, Vivian found it easier to sleep that night than she had in quite some time. If Lord Winter had cared enough to save her, he was not the villainous Lord Lucifer—he was the man she had fallen in love with.

Chapter Fifteen

Ignoring her mother's protests, Vivian was up the next morning, determined that she and Tom would get on about their business. Mrs. Reddington, knowing nothing of course of their concerns, was horrified by her daughter's decision and did her best to confine her to her chamber. Recognizing a losing proposition, she finally compromised by telling Vivian that Tom must accompany her everywhere she went in case she became faint. Since they had planned to look into some matters together—and since Tom had already informed Vivian that she wasn't getting out of his sight—neither of them had any fault to find with this ruling.

The first thing they did was to collect the snuff box. To Tom's infinite relief it was precisely where Vivian had left it: deep in a barrel of oats in the stable. He was prepared to quibble about the wisdom of her hiding place when he looked at her expression and, anticipating an ugly battle which neither of them would win, heroically overcame his impulse to criticize her. It was because of this that they were able to amicably ride

into Lynhurst together, arriving with no rift between them—
as yet.

They had come, as Tom so elegantly stated it, "to nose
around" in the hope of turning up some bit of information
about Roger Wilding that might help them.

"Well, you must remember, Tom, not to mention Drake's
name. Do please remember that as far as anyone knows, he is
with Wellington where he should be."

"What sort of rattlebrain do you think I am, Viv?" he asked
crossly. "Do you think that I'm going to barge up and down
High Street asking after Drake Reddington?"

"Perhaps not," she replied, after a moment or two of reflection, "but I wouldn't swear that you're not capable of doing
precisely that. Just remember that we could interfere with something very important if we do make a mistake."

"I must say that you're a pretty one to be telling me about
making a mistake," Tom continued, still miffed because of her
attitude. "This is Little Miss Muffet who published the most
scandalous story possible about her own fiancé."

"That isn't fair, Tom!" she said shortly, her face flaming.
"You know that it was Lacey who actually did so." To her
horror, she could feel tears welling. "I wouldn't have harmed
Lord Winter," she continued, as they began to spill hotly down
her cheeks.

"Oh, all right, Viv! Don't turn into a watering pot! I'm
sorry—I'll cry craven and give over teasing you."

By the time they entered the village, they had made their
peace and were prepared to look about them in good earnest,
watching for anything that might help them with their enigma.
Vivian had not yet told Tom about Lord Winter's presence in
the area, nor of the fact that he had been present at her attack,
but she was planning to keep her eyes open for that gentleman
as well.

Lynhurst appeared very quiet. They called at the draper's

shop to make a purchase for Mrs. Reddington, and fell into gossiping with the clerk, who was finding time hanging heavy on her hands.

"There isn't much excitement in town this week, is there, Mrs. Dott?" inquired Tom casually, leaning against the counter and acting as though he had nothing in particular upon his mind. It was a pose that Vivian had informed him came naturally to him.

"Ah, there's more here than meets the eye, Mr. Cane," replied Mrs. Dott, taking umbrage at this aspersion cast upon the good name of Lynhurst. "It isn't only in London that out-of-the-way things happen."

"Indeed?" asked Tom, looking at her with interest. "What has been going on then?"

"It's that poor young man that came down from London and stayed at The Golden Boar. Such a lovely man to look at, he was—dressed to the nines, he did, just purchased a pair of handsome gloves of York tan from the shop next door—and now he's dead. He's the one what went over the edge of the cliff this Wednesday past. Dead as a doornail he was, before they ever got him back to the inn. Didn't even have time for any last words, more's the pity."

Tom and Vivian made the appropriate clucking sounds and, thus encouraged, Mrs. Dott continued her tale, her eyes bright. "But that's not the worst of it," she said in a low voice, leaning toward them. "They can't locate his body!"

"No!" exclaimed Vivian. "Do you mean that he was taken from his room?"

Mrs. Dott nodded darkly. "Who's to say for what reasons he was taken? There's not a soul hereabouts but has taken to locking his door at nights now."

"But to have lost his body!" exclaimed Vivian in horror. "How terrible for his family!"

"Just what I said myself," Mrs. Dott said, giving her an

approving look. The two young people were supplying her with a most satisfying audience. "Although none of his people have been down to try to look into the matter."

"What did the inn do with his things?" asked Vivian.

"That's another very strange thing," said Mrs. Dott darkly. "They're nowhere to be found."

Tom and Vivian again made the appropriate sounds indicative of interest, glancing at one another briefly.

"I suppose you heard that Mr. Wilding rode out to Trevelyan to pay his respects to my family," commented Vivian.

Mrs. Dott nodded eagerly, hopeful for additional gossip.

"He seemed in very good spirits, but a messenger rode out from The Golden Boar and his mood seemed to change very quickly."

"No doubt," nodded Mrs. Dott knowingly. "I heard tell that the message was about a dear friend of his—no names given, of course—who sent for him, telling him that it was a matter of life and death."

She paused a moment for dramatic effect, then added slowly, "And, of course, for him it most truly was."

Tom and Vivian nodded their heads in agreement, signifying that they were at a loss for words. Satisfied by their reaction, Mrs. Dott left them for a moment to attend to another client. Tom and Vivian were engaged in a quiet conversation when she happened to glance at the other customer. She gave a quiet gasp and her companion looked up sharply to see what was amiss.

Their eyes met, although they said nothing. The other customer was Mrs. Connaught. She appeared not to notice them, and they slipped quietly from the shop, Tom promising himself to revisit it soon. Vivian's head was again awhirl. What could have brought Lady Connaught here except Lord Winter? That thought in itself was agitating, but she had to consider the matter of Mr. Wilding's disappearance, too, which had occurred

because of the fact he was too involved in Drake's affairs—
how was Drake connected to all of this? Was he the friend
who had sent the life-and-death message to poor Mr. Wilding?
Or had someone sent him the message using Drake's name?

Fortunately, they saw nothing of either Lord Winter or Drake
as they made their way through town, but they also turned up
very little additional information of value about Wilding. They
had been trying to come up with a list of places that Wilding
might have been spirited away to, and they were most unhappy
with the wide array of possibilities.

"Depends very much upon who has taken him, of course,"
said Tom in a low voice as they ate their nuncheon at a small
shop.

"And upon whether or not the poor man is still alive,"
whispered Vivian.

Tom nodded somberly. "And if it's Hawkins who is responsible, he was probably taken to Grassmere—and more than
likely he's dead by now."

Vivian shuddered briefly. Just the name of the man was
enough to give her a chill. He had no conscience at all, so poor
Mr. Wilding would indeed have had no chance with him.

"Even if he were still alive and at Grassmere, we couldn't
get to him," she said, still whispering. Recent events had made
both of them more cautious.

Tom nodded grimly. "It's possible that Drake might know
something of his whereabouts, but that'll do us no good because
we can't get in touch with him."

"Well, if Drake knows where he is, he will do all that he
can to protect and help him," replied Vivian confidently.

"Who else might have taken him?" asked Tom, his brow
furrowed with the effort of thinking this matter through to its
logical conclusion.

"Possibly whoever that snuff box belongs to," responded
Vivian. "And we have no way of knowing that."

Tom nodded dismally.

"And, Tom," Vivian added, glancing about to make certain that no one was close enough to hear them or to see what she was taking from her pocket, "I've had an idea about the key word to unlock the cipher."

His eyes brightened and he waited for her response. Any step forward at the moment would be helpful.

"Butterfly," she whispered.

"Of course!" he exclaimed. "You've hit upon it, Viv! I'm certain of it!"

In his excitement, he had forgotten to speak quietly, and a man seated at a table several feet away looked up at them curiously.

"Tom, you idiot!" Vivian whispered. "Keep your voice down. There's no need to share it with all of Lynhurst."

She slipped her hand back into her pocket. "We'll try this at home," she said. "There's no need in attracting more attention to ourselves."

The two of them rode back to Trevelyan, watching carefully for any sign of trouble all the way, but their journey was uneventful. Tom appeared almost disappointed, but Vivian, after the troubles of the day before, was deeply grateful. Her head had begun to throb, and she gave way to her mother's pleas that she lie down and rest before dinner.

She had one more thing she wished to do, however, and she sat down to her little lap desk and wrote a note to Ben. Unlike many of his cronies, he was a literate man and took pleasure in his newspapers. Folding it tightly and sealing it, Vivian slipped down the servants' stairs so that she wouldn't attract anyone's attention, and out to the stable, where she handed Joe the note and asked him to deliver it to Ben at The Lighthouse.

She had wanted very badly to ask about Drake, but she hadn't dared to. So great a case had he made for secrecy that she did not dare to do anything to upset things, even though she knew that Ben was well aware of his presence. She contented herself with alluding to "taking good care of any guests that he might have at the inn," and asking him to indicate a good time that he could meet her at "the drawing room" tonight. She knew that he would understand immediately where she meant. The largest and grandest of the caves he used for storage they had frequently referred to by that nickname. She had full confidence in Ben—he would be there.

She would try to decipher the note in the snuff box after she had slept a little to clear her head. Stirring the powder the doctor had given her for the headache into her water, she drank it, eager to have back her usual sharpness of mind. Certain that she had done all that she could for the moment, she lay down for her nap, the snuff box and its contents safely under her pillow.

It was almost dinnertime when Lacey's scratch at the door awakened her. "I did not realize that you were not just barging right in anymore," she said dryly as Lacey perched on the edge of her bed.

"You always know how to say the thing to make a person feel right at home," her cousin replied coolly.

"You flatter me," Vivian replied, her voice a shade chillier.

Dinner was almost as warm and comfortable as their preliminary conversation, for Mrs. Reddington was still depressed by Mr. Wilding's death, and Tom felt most unwell, probably as a result of the oysters he had dined upon at their nuncheon.

"I told you it wasn't wise to eat oysters this month," Vivian reminded him, and he darted her a brief, red-eyed glance and remained in a vacuum of pained silence for the duration of dinner. Tom's indisposition had at least one advantage, she reflected comfortably. He would not be troubling her that evening, and she could take herself off to meet Ben without fear of interference. Before leaving, she found a safe hiding place for the snuff box. If Tom were right and someone might be watching for them in order to take it, she would not be foolish enough to carry it out with her tonight.

Instead, she went to a secret place on the shelves of the library. Her father had had a small section of false-front books fitted snugly into a shelf just above the eye level of a good-sized man. Behind them was a place for securing small valuables or private papers. So far as she knew, no one except Drake and herself knew about it. Their father had put it in place after John had left home and taken up his residence in Scotland and his flat in London, and Mrs. Reddington considered the library sacred ground, first for her husband and then for Vivian. Climbing up on a ladder, she put the box securely in place, wrapped in a dark piece of felt.

The evening was damp and cold, and Vivian wrapped herself more closely in her cloak as she and Pimm picked their way carefully to The Drawing Room. She was anxious to confide in Ben, and to try to discover what he knew of the curious matters that seemed to be hemming them in on every side. Too, she wanted to ask why he had not managed to unite the gentlemen against the likes of James Hawkins.

Leaving Pimm, Vivian made her way carefully down a rocky path to the mouth of The Drawing Room. The night was dark and the wind gusty, sending wraith-like clouds hurrying across the face of the pale moon. She had not gone far when she saw on the distant waters a single light flashing from a ship. From below her there was an answering flash. Freezing in place, Vivian crouched against the cliff, wrapping her dark woollen cloak about her, the hood pulled down, and waited to see what would happen next.

She did not have to wait long. Soon a longboat was pulled up onto the beach below them, and two or three dark figures got out. She watched carefully, expecting them to begin to unload some of their goods quickly onto the beach. Instead, two figures melted away from the darkness below her and made their way toward the longboat. The walk and height of one of them was unmistakable. It was Lord Winter. Holding her breath, she waited, wondering what his business was with these people.

They held a brief colloquy on the sandy strip next to the water, with Winter occasionally gesturing back toward the cliffs. One of the men he was talking with appeared to be very strong in his opinions. Even at this distance and in the darkness, Vivian could distinguish the way in which he shook his head and, finally, threw something to the beach before turning and placing himself again in the longboat.

Lord Winter, however, seemed dissatisfied with that move, striding over to jerk the man from the boat and fling him onto the beach. She could not hear their voices above the pounding of the waves against the rocks, but she was sure there was loud conversation taking place. One of the men with Winter ran to the side of the man lying on the beach and helped him to his feet. The third figure in the longboat suddenly stood, holding out a hand toward Lord Winter.

To her surprise, he turned back to the longboat and took the extended hand, helping the figure from the boat. In so doing the hood of the cloaked figure fell back and Vivian gasped. It was Lady Connaught. The moonlight glinted on her dark hair as she threw her arms about Lord Winter's neck. He neither held her nor repulsed her. He appeared simply to submit to her embrace.

Vivian was about halfway between the top of the cliff and the mouth of The Drawing Room, and she decided that she would risk going on. If she went back to Pimm, she would have to go home in defeat, knowing no more than she did right now. And she *very* much wanted to know what was going on— and how her fiancé and her brother were involved.

An argument appeared to rise very suddenly between two of the figures on the shore, and a brief bout of fisticuffs ensued, which Lord Winter quickly called to a halt. Taking advantage of the distraction, Vivian hurried into the mouth of the cave, where a lantern, partially darkened, sat upon a keg of brandy. Moving quickly into the shadows beyond it, she settled down to wait and to observe.

She did not have to wait long. Lady Connaught entered first, shaking out her long dark hair.

"Have you truly no feeling for me any longer, Richard?" she asked in a throaty voice, turning suddenly and pulling him toward her. She lifted one of his hands and held it against her cheek. "My skin is still as soft, my hair still as silky as it was when you could not go a day—nay, an hour—without holding me."

She took his hand, still limp and lifeless, and held it to her hair, the palm stroking the length of it. "How can you say that has all gone, Richard?" she asked him in a low voice. "Such feelings do not suddenly cease—you are simply no longer admitting them."

Lord Winter moved away from her, into the light where Vivian could see his face. To her relief, he did not look passionate, but mildly—and cynically—amused.

"What are you after now, Rachel?" he inquired. "You would not go to so much trouble for nothing. And I see that you've taken a trip to Paris, too."

Vivian held her breath. To Paris! Lady Connaught was a spy for Bonaparte! What did that make Lord Winter? Surely not a spy, too, she told herself, watching his reaction to the dark beauty before him.

"What can I offer you, Rachel, that you don't already possess?" he asked.

"Why, you yourself, Richard," she replied, smiling up at him and speaking in a husky, almost masculine voice.

"Not my fortune?" he asked, his voice light.

"No, of course not!" she exclaimed, drawing closer and

again putting her arms about his neck and pulling his face down to hers. "How can you think me so mercenary, Richard?"

He laughed, and his laughter acted like a pail of cold water tossed upon the lady. She pulled away from him and glared up into his eyes.

He appeared unaffected, and his laughter continued unabated. Straightening her shoulders, Lady Connaught turned from him without a word and disappeared into the darkness outside the cave.

Vivian sat and watched Lord Winter. He laughed for a minute or two more, then lapsed into silence, glancing about the cave and then outside, walking to its mouth and staring off into the distance.

It was Drake who entered next. Without realizing it, Vivian had retreated deeper and deeper into the cave, careful to keep herself beyond the reach of the light, sinking at last behind a large boulder that offered some protection both from the light and from any searching eyes. Concentrating as she was on Drake, it was difficult to keep from shrieking aloud when she realized that she had stepped upon a human body lying behind her on the floor of the cave.

Chapter Sixteen

Sinking to her knees, Vivian tried to see through the thick darkness behind her. She ran her hands lightly over the face she encountered, and discovered that a bandana had been wrapped tightly against the lower part to keep the person from crying out. Leaning close so that she could not be heard by anyone else, she whispered, "Mr. Wilding?"

There was immediate nodding and twitching from the body that lay bound and gagged. In a wave of relief, she knew that Roger Wilding had survived his ordeal and that Drake's friend had not been done to death by any miscreants. She heaved a sigh of relief but, realizing the danger in which they both now lay, she leaned close to his ear and whispered softly, "Don't move at all, Mr. Wilding. There are smugglers here—and Lord Winter. Don't draw attention to us."

Mr. Wilding immediately lay as one dead, so she knew she need have no fear that he would betray them. Settling herself carefully, she prepared to watch what came next. To her dismay, however, there was a sudden outcry from beyond the mouth of The Drawing Room. She could hear the sounds of movement, an occasional shot and scream—and then there was nothing.

Looking carefully over the top of her sheltering rock, Vivian took stock of the situation. No bodies lay on the floor of the cave beside the lantern. The lantern itself had tumbled to the ground, its one unshuttered side casting a golden glow on the wall of the cave, her shadow making crazy, ghostly shapes as she moved past it. Outside everything seemed quiet. She saw no people, no horses, no boats. All was still—and watchful.

Watchful herself, she made no sudden moves. Instead, she settled beside the recumbent Mr. Wilding, after assuring him in a whisper that all was well and that as soon as she could be sure they were alone, she would untie him. They sat perfectly still for what she estimated to be an hour. Having heard no sound in all that time, she set about the business of releasing poor Mr. Wilding.

Using Drake's knife, which she always kept with her, she cut through the ropes that bound his wrists and ankles, moving slowly and carefully to avoid doing damage to the unfortunate victim. Once assured that all was well, she managed to unknot the gag and helped him to chafe his wrists and ankles so that the blood began to circulate once more.

"Don't say anything," she had cautioned him in a whisper as she removed the gag. "We can't be certain that they have all gone. Don't speak until we are safely back at Trevelyan."

She felt his head nod convulsively and knew that she would have no lack of cooperation from Mr. Wilding. Mystified by the whole evening, but being very careful of the victim, she carefully closed the one open side of the lantern, darkening the cave.

"Now we won't be visible to anyone outside as we leave," she explained softly, taking his hand and leading him toward the mouth of the cave.

It took them some time to reach the top of the cliff and

Pimm, for Mr. Wilding scarcely had command of his limbs, so long had he lain bound and gagged. Vivian guided him carefully, keeping him on the inside of the narrow path that led to the top. Watch as she would, she could see no sign of anyone else aside from themselves. The longboat was gone, and if a ship lay at anchor close by, it could not be seen. There was no sign of movement on the beach below or on the cliff path above, and no sound reached them but the sound of the waves.

When they reached Pimm, Vivian helped Mr. Wilding to mount. When he showed signs of wanting her to ride instead of him, she whispered that it would take them three times as long to reach home and safety if she rode; whereupon Mr. Wilding said no more, but clung gratefully to the saddle while Vivian walked them home through the quiet night, watching carefully for anything that seemed odd or out of place.

Happily, they soon reached Trevelyan, and as they drew within view of the house, Vivian dared to turn and ask her guest a question.

"Mr. Wilding," she inquired, her voice trembling, "who set upon you and tied you up?"

"Lord Winter," he answered. "I am sorry to tell you, Miss Reddington, but the stories are all true. It was Winter who threw me from my horse and Winter who bound and gagged me and left me in that cave to die."

Vivian did not disabuse him of this notion, for she knew that he could scarcely have died there, so often was it the meeting place of some of the brotherhood. And yet it must have felt so to him—and possibly Winter would have known no better than to leave him, thinking that he would indeed die. Still, she found it impossible to accept that this could be true. Lord Winter was, she thought, too good a man than to have done such a thing—and yet Mr. Wilding had no reason to lie and every reason to tell the truth.

She found that she could not help herself. The tears began to slide unbidden down her cheeks. "I am very sorry for your trouble, Mr. Wilding—and sorry that I have been at least partially responsible in bringing it down upon you."

"Not responsible," he protested, raising a weary hand. "Not at all—don't think it for a moment. You have saved me, Miss Reddington, and kept me from a lingering death in that cold, damp cave."

"You will soon be home in a warm bed, recovering from your accident," she said soothingly.

She stopped for just a moment and looked back at him, perched precariously upon the weary Pimm. "Mr. Wilding, did you see Drake again?" she asked. "After you got the snuff box and the note?"

He shook his head. "Don't know what happened to the old boy," he said regretfully. "Hope he isn't in a hobble because he's keeping the wrong company," he added. "Hanging about with that devil Winter, you know—and some other unsavory character with too many teeth."

Knowing that he was referring to smiling James Hawkins, Vivian could feel herself smiling—something that she hadn't done for a while. James Hawkins undeniably was the possessor of too many teeth, all of them white and all of them sharp. "Puts one in mind of a weasel," observed Wilding, when discussing him later.

When they arrived at Trevelyan, Vivian let them in, locked the doors again, and placed Mr. Wilding securely in the darkened library. "I'll just run up and get Tom," she told him. "Then he'll help get you off to bed."

She started for the door, then thought better of it and came back to her father's crystal decanter and poured him a generous glass of brandy. "You've had a terrible chill," she said to Mr. Wilding, handing it to him with a smile.

Vivian left him smiling beatifically into the glass, scarcely able to realize that his nightmare was over. His joints ached, his bones ached, his head ached, and he was cold from head to toe—but he was alive. The warmth and bracing bite of the brandy strengthened him and he sat a little straighter. "French," he murmured blissfully.

Getting Tom into motion proved to be a bit more taxing than she had anticipated. Tiptoeing into his chamber, she placed her candle on his nightstand and shook him by the shoulder. He moved and made incoherent sounds, but he did not open his eyes.

"Tom!" she whispered sharply, her hand on his shoulder less gentle. "Wake up, Tom!"

Far from waking up, he settled more deeply among the covers, snoring loudly. Her patience worn by her long, tiring evening and her throbbing forehead, she smiled as her gaze settled upon the pitcher on his nightstand. The thought occurred and she did not resist it: she lifted the pitcher and poured it over his neck and shoulders, bringing him sputtering to life.

"What the devil!" he shouted, surfacing from the flood. He scrubbed at his soaking face and hair with his sheet and gazed up angrily at his tormentor.

"I say, Viv! Wound or no wound, my girl, you're going to pay for this one!" He appeared prepared to make good on his threat immediately, but she raised her hand in warning.

"Don't be so loud, Tom. You'll bring the household down upon us."

"What do I care about that?" he demanded. "I'm damned well not the one creeping about in the middle of the night pouring water upon innocent sleepers! It's enough to send someone into a fit, Viv!"

"Aren't you going to ask me why I did it?" she asked.

He glared at her. "I've never known you to need a reason to do something outrageous." He paused a moment or two, then added, "Oh, very well. Why did you do it, Viv? Why try to drown me in my sleep?"

"I needed to wake you up," she explained patiently.

"And you thought this would be the way that would work out the best?" he asked in disbelief. "What's wrong with simply saying 'Wake up, Tom. I need you'?"

"Nothing at all—except that it didn't work," she responded.

"Oh, as though you tried it!" Tom exclaimed, trying to towel dry his hair and shoulders in the frigid room.

Trying to be helpful, Vivian moved to the hearth to kindle the banked embers. "I did!" she said indignantly. "And all you did was snore more loudly and twist the covers about you!"

Unconvinced, he continued to towel briskly.

"Aren't you going to ask me why I wanted you to wake up?" she asked. "You really have no proper curiosity or imagination, Tom."

Stung by these aspersions, he said acidly, "Go ahead and tell me everything you wish to say, Viv, and stop baiting me with questions. What did you wish to tell me?"

"I have Mr. Wilding in the library," she responded simply.

Tom sat down where the chair by the fire should have been. It was not, and so he landed flatly on the floor, still staring at her.

"You're bamming me, Viv," he said, his eyes wide—whether with pain or disbelief she was uncertain.

Vivian shook her head. "He's here—a little the worse for wear after being tied up and gagged all this time—but here."

"Tied up and gagged?" Tom asked. "Do you mean to tell me that someone actually did kidnap Wilding? That it wasn't just our imagination?"

Vivian shook her head. "It was real. I found him in a cave along the shore."

"You found him *where,* Vivian Reddington?" he asked, his

tone ominous. "Do you mean to tell me that I cannot get ill without your taking advantage of the situation to go off to some godforsaken place when I've warned you not even to leave the house?"

She nodded. "I suppose that's true, Tom. You can't. I don't want to stay cooped up in the house—and I won't, you know."

"I suppose I do," he sighed. "Well, at least you're here in one piece," he said. "Though no thanks to you, I'm sure."

He studied her for a moment. "Well, what are we to do now?"

"We'll go down and get Mr. Wilding, and then we'll take him away to one of the guest chambers in the old wing. You need to help him get settled so that he can get a comfortable night's rest after his long ordeal."

"What of *my* ordeal?" demanded Tom.

Vivian looked thoughtful. "Well, you could make up a pallet in Mr. Wilding's chamber," she mused. "That would be wise, I think. Then we could be certain that no one tried to harm him again."

"You haven't told me who tried to harm him this time," complained Tom. "Who did it?"

Vivian turned her head away. "Mr. Wilding says that Lord Winter was responsible," she said in a low voice. "He said that Winter bound him and left him for dead."

Tom looked at her in disbelief. "Winter?" he exclaimed "What would Winter be doing down here and why would he do such a farfetched thing?"

Then he thought about Vivian's book. "Do you mean to say, Viv," he said in a low voice, "that any of your book was accurate? Does Winter really work with smugglers? . . . and with spies?"

"It seems to appear that way to Mr. Wilding," she responded unhappily. "Let's not talk of that now, Tom," she said. "Let's go down to the library and get poor Mr. Wilding to a warm bed.''

Tom followed her, hoping that getting their guest to bed would be a comparatively easy matter. They did not wish to alert any of the household and would use a distant unused guest chamber that the servants would not be likely to notice. Tom would have to lay the fire and Vivian would make the bed.

They set to work industriously, and it was not long until they had him safely stowed in bed, one of Tom's nightcaps perched atop his head, several blankets tucked about him, a warm fire blazing, and a decanter of brandy at his bedside. Mr. Wilding required no more of life. He smiled gently and bade them both good night, assuring them that he was very comfortable now.

''Sleep as long as you like, Mr. Wilding,'' Vivian told him, ''but remember that you shouldn't walk about because everyone thinks that you are dead. Tom or I will bring you your food and anything else that you need.''

It was, however, too late to address her guest. Mr. Wilding was already deeply asleep. The events of the past two days had been too much for him.

Tom settled himself on a pallet by the fire and Vivian made her way back to her chamber, almost too weary to find her way. She was too tired to notice that the door of Lacey's chamber was ajar and that it closed softly as she walked by.

Chapter Seventeen

So tired was Vivian that she slept late the next morning, something that she almost never did. When she did awaken and realized the time, she hurriedly dressed and made her way quietly to Mr. Wilding's distant chamber. She scratched lightly on the door and then let herself in. Both gentlemen were still sound asleep, Tom curled on the pallet in front of a dying fire.

It took a bit of fancy footwork, but Vivian was able to raid the pantry and assemble a tray for the two gentlemen without attracting attention, and to sneak up the servants' stairs to Mr. Wilding's chamber without attracting a soul. She awoke Tom and hurried him back to his own room so that his absence wouldn't arouse undue attention.

"There is no problem about why you didn't sleep in your chamber last night, Tom," she said pointedly. "All you need do is to comment that you were about to shave and dropped the pitcher of water on your bed, so you had to find another place to sleep."

"Thank you very much, Vivian," he responded bitterly.

"You who know so very much about shaving. Why was I shaving just before I went to bed? And where did I sleep? I'll cut a pretty figure—and all because of you."

"Don't get on your high ropes, Tom," she responded briskly. "We have more important matters to attend to."

"And what do you mean by that?" he asked suspiciously. "Which matters are we attending to?"

"Remember the butterfly, Tom?" she inquired.

He looked blank for a moment, then the light dawned upon him, and he leaned toward her eagerly. "I say, yes I do, Viv. I think that we ought to look into that matter immediately."

And together the two of them retired to the library, where Tom watched the door while Vivian retrieved the snuff box and took out the cipher. A few minutes of concentration were unfortunately enough to show her that "butterfly" was not the key word needed for this particular cipher.

"It's too bad, Viv," said Tom comfortingly. "It was an excellent notion, you know. It should have worked if Drake had been using his wits when he put this note in the butterfly box."

Vivian smiled at him a moment, appreciating his support, but she was too discouraged to comment. She had been so certain that she was right.

Tom was still poking the note about, as though to unearth any secrets it might contain. "If, of course, Drake is the one responsible for writing the note," he added as an afterthought. "*Is* this Drake's handwriting, Viv?"

She stared at him a moment and then leaped from her chair and hugged him. "I never would have allowed it to be true, Thomas Cane, but you are a genius! No, this isn't Drake's handwriting! And so of course the key word might not be 'butterfly' even if it *was* butterfly!"

Tom looked at her blankly. "Slowly, Viv, slowly. What are you talking about?"

"It's as simple as pie," she responded, smiling as she scribbled rapidly on the sheet of foolscap before her. "It could be French. We needed to try the French word for 'butterfly.'"

"We did?" asked Tom, bemused.

"Yes—*papillon*," she replied. "Didn't you learn anything from Crewett?"

"Of course, I did," responded Tom with dignity. "But French was very difficult for me since I couldn't very well take the Grand Tour with Boney marching all over Europe. And so how was I to learn to speak like the Frogs if I couldn't visit there and hear them speaking it?"

"Tom, you are hopeless," she said, still scribbling wildly.

When she laid down her pen, there was a brief silence while Tom watched her.

"Well?" he said finally, weary of waiting for some sort of reaction as she stared down at the paper before her.

"We've got it, Tom!" she exclaimed. "I don't know just *what* we've got, but we've got something."

"Show me, Viv!" he demanded, and they both bent their heads over over Vivian's papers while she explained.

"Look at this, Tom. It's simple."

"Well, it doesn't look it, Viv! I mean, who would know what *aogl ltbgtr* is supposed to mean?"

"That says 'Lord Winter,'" she told him. "I thought perhaps this might all be written in French, but it isn't."

Tom turned to stare at her. "Is that the truth, Viv, or are you bamboozling me? It says 'Lord Winter'?"

"It's the truth," she assured him. "And it's simple enough to decipher when you have this table. This is the one I told you about. A Frenchman came up with it a couple of hundred years ago."

And she put a copy of the Vigenère Tableau in front of him beside the note from the snuff box. Under each letter of the note she had printed a letter from the word *papillon*, beginning over again as many times as she needed to and beginning at the beginning each time she started a new sentence.

Tracing across the top of the table, she found the letter *p,* the first letter of *papillon,* and traced down the column of letters under the *p* until she found *a,* the first letter of the ciphered message. Then she traced it to the parallel letter running down the lefthand side of the table—which was *L.*

"So, you see, using *papillon* as a key gives us 'Lord Winter.' "

"Well, what does the rest of it say, Viv? Read it to me."

"It says: *Lord Winter and his brother Richard are my emissaries. Present to the Bank of London. Madame Papillon.*"

Tom stared at her. "And what does that mean?" he asked. "Who is Madame Papillon?"

"I have no idea. And notice that the present Lord Winter's name *is* Richard," she pointed out to him. "This refers to him as the brother of Lord Winter."

"So this was written twenty years ago," Tom said in wonder. "It has been that long since he killed his brother—at least according to what they were saying in the clubs," he added hurriedly, seeing her expression.

"We don't know that he did any such thing!" returned Vivian sharply. "The important question is who Madame Papillon is and what they were to do for her at the Bank of London."

Tom shook his head. "Can't say without going there," he responded. "I daresay we should look into the matter, though."

"Of course we should," she snapped. "What I would like to know, though, is how this came into Drake's hands and why it's so important to him."

"Well, just think, Viv. It has Winter's name, doesn't it?"

She nodded slowly. "So? What are you saying, Tom?"

"That, according to your book and half of London, Winter is a smuggler and a spy for the French. Naturally Drake would be interested. Do you think he knows what the note says?"

"I have no idea, Tom" she replied. "I should think, though, that if I deciphered it, Drake could, too, if he had enough time to examine it—except, of course, I had the advantage of Papa's books to help me."

They sat there in silence for a few minutes and then Tom grew restive.

"What do you think we should do now, Viv?" he inquired. "We have the note, and the box, of course. What comes next?"

Vivian had been considering the situation seriously. "I believe, Tom," she answered thoughtfully, "that we should go riding this afternoon and you should meet a friend of mine."

"This don't seem to me the best time for a social call, Viv," he protested. "What are we going to do about all of the rest of this?" And he gestured toward the note.

"This isn't a social call, Tom, and you have to promise me solemnly that you will never say a word about it."

Tom began to look apprehensive. "I don't know, Viv. I think that I should know a little more about just what you're getting me into before I commit myself to a promise." Years of childhood experience had made him very cautious where promises to Vivian were concerned. Too often they required him to do something painful or embarrassing or difficult.

"Then I won't take you," she said decisively, moving toward the door. "I shall see you later in the day."

"Oh, very well!" he snapped. "You know I'm not likely to allow you to go riding off by yourself after all that's happened. It's plain as a pikestaff that you would come back laid out on a shutter if I were to let you go."

She smiled. "I knew you wouldn't let me down, Tom!" she exclaimed brightly, coming back to take his hand.

"Well, isn't that a charming picture," drawled Lacey.

They both looked up in surprise to see her standing in the doorway of the library. Behind her stood John. Vivian dropped Tom's hand and looked at them.

"Hello, John," she said casually. "How surprising to see you here. I should think that Trevelyan was too boring for you."

"No, Vivian, strangely enough, I find quite a few things to occupy myself aside from attending one ball after another. I manage to remain busy—and quite happy."

"You may remain busy, John," she agreed, "but I think you must agree that Eustacia stays even busier."

Lacey flushed, but Vivian's sarcasm was lost upon John. "Yes, I know that Lacey keeps a busy schedule," he said, "which is all the more reason for me to be impressed with the manner in which she has kept me informed of your activities. Unfortunately, she has just been telling me that some of your evening activities are not particularly socially acceptable ones."

"Do you mean my being in Tom's chamber, Lacey?" she inquired casually, ignoring her brother's pained expression.

"Yes, I do," she said stiffly. "Someone has to look after you, Vivian, if you refuse to be sensible yourself."

"It seems to me, Eustacia," said Mrs. Reddington from the doorway where she had been listening, her anger rising, "that if Vivian needs someone to look after her, I am the logical person to come to."

John bowed in the general direction of his mother. "And that would be true, madam, if you would do so. However, since you allow her to run wild, as she always has, someone else—like myself—must step in."

"What a bag of moonshine!" scoffed Tom . "Just as though you could keep a rein on her, Reddington! When have you ever been able to do so?"

John flushed angrily. "This is a family matter, Mr. Cane—and, although you don't seem to realize it, you are *not* family."

Tom started toward the door, but Vivian was ahead of him. "Aside from thinking too well of yourself, John," she said over her shoulder, "you have shockingly bad manners. That is scarcely the way to treat a guest."

"Vivian! Come back here this instant!" he called after her. "I forbid you to leave this room!"

He was, however, speaking to the empty air. Vivian had departed and Tom followed in her wake.

Mrs. Reddington looked at him with raised brows. "You handled that very well indeed, John," she said. "Now that you have shown me how to manage Vivian and how to treat our guests, I am certain that I will have no trouble at all." And nodding her head gracefully, she also left the library, leaving Lacey and John in full possession of it.

Vivian had moved quickly—too quickly for Tom. He hurried up the stairs to her chamber, but she was not there. Puzzled, he turned back to retrace his steps and try to discover her whereabouts.

Chapter Eighteen

When John arrived, Vivian had decided against taking the risk of introducing Tom to Ben and The Lighthouse. Instead, she headed there alone, Pimm trotting along the path as though he sensed her need to hurry. Joe had not been in the stable to help her with Pimm, so she hadn't been able to question him about delivering the note to Ben yesterday. She was still puzzled about why Ben had allowed her to arrive at The Drawing Room when they were expecting a shipment. As protective as he had always been of her, that was very out of character for him. Nor had she seen him at any time during the evening. The more she thought of it, the more troubled she grew.

When she tethered Pimm at the base of The Lighthouse, she was very cautious. Everything appeared to be much the same as usual and as she let herself into the hidden cellar, she began to feel that perhaps she had made too much of all this and that there was no need to take the risk of putting on her costume and masquerading one last time as Ben's "nevvy." As she lighted the candle, she heard a slight movement behind her and whirled about.

"Miss Reddington, I believe," said James Hawkins, bowing and flashing the teeth that Mr. Wilding had commented upon in an unpleasantly carnivorous smile. "We have not had the pleasure of meeting formally, so allow me to introduce myself."

"There is no need, Mr. Hawkins," she said coolly. "Like everyone else along this part of the coast, I know who you are."

He smiled again. "You flatter me, ma'am."

"I'm sorry," she said, looking at him in the distant, disdainful manner that one might use in examining a bug scuttling across the floor. "I did not intend to."

A sharp groan from the darkness caught her attention, so she did not notice that Hawkins's smile faded rapidly to a snarl. Holding the candle high, she hurried in the direction of the sound. There she found what she had feared. Ben lay there, bound and gagged—and unconscious. But it was not Ben who had groaned. It was Drake.

Remembering that his idenitity was a secret, she gave no sign of recognition, bending instead over the recumbent figure of Marley.

"This man needs a surgeon," she said sharply, examining a wound on Ben's forehead that had dried to a dark, brownish stain.

"Forgive me, Miss Reddington," said Hawkins, once more smiling. "I am afraid that we will have to do without such niceties. A surgeon would ask unwelcome questions. And, of course," he added thoughtfully, "asking one to come would indicate that I have some desire to see Marley recover."

Vivian favored him with a brief, searing glance, then bent over her friend. She took a handkerchief from her pocket and pulled a flask from an inside pocket of Ben's jacket, opening it quickly and soaking the linen square with brandy, then applying it carefully to the wound to clean it. Ben stirred at the sharp stinging and his eyes flickered open. When he managed to focus on her, they opened even more widely and he looked frightened.

"Yes, Ben, I know that I'm where I shouldn't be again," she said comfortingly, "but never you mind. I'll get you set to rights and then we'll deal with the problem at hand."

"How charming," drawled Hawkins, who had been watching all of this with great interest. "I have never heard myself referred to as 'the problem at hand'—particularly when I am standing next to the speaker. You charm me, dear lady."

Vivian, transparent as always, flashed him a glance of loathing. "I do not mean to, Mr. Hawkins," she said sharply. "I mean to accuse you, and if possible—and I am not sure it *is* possible—to insult you."

Hawkins threw her an ugly glance, and Drake groaned warningly.

"You had best listen to the other gentleman, Miss Reddington," he said. "It is best not to cross me."

"I am terrified," she assured him, continuing to clean Ben's wound while looking straight at Drake. "Everyone knows that you are a man to be feared, and I can see that."

"Can you indeed?" he inquired, his voice pleased. This, his tone seemed to say, was more the attitude that he felt his due. "I believe that I am not without a certain physical presence that impresses."

"I merely meant, Mr. Hawkins, that anyone who must tie up his enemies rather than face them on equal ground is a man to be feared. He is not a gentleman and does not abide by the rules that bind more honorable men."

Drake's eyes were almost starting from his head as he attempted to engage her attention and signal to her to stop talking in such a manner. She gave her brother a brief, reassuring nod and a pat on the shoulder, then turned back to Hawkins.

"Look at this gentleman, for instance," she said, gesturing to Drake. "I don't know why you have chosen to bind him hand and foot, but you must fear him—and Ben—to bind them so closely. You surprise me, sir. After all the tales I have heard of how fearful a figure you are, here you are, taking base advantage of two men, one of them badly wounded. I should have thought you would be a man for duels and hand-to-hand combat rather than treachery."

"I had heard that you were wild, Miss Reddington," said Hawkins, a little thickly, "wild to a fault, indeed, but I had never heard anyone say that you had such a shrewish tongue."

"You must have encountered people who do not know me well," she said briskly. "I am as I have always been. I tell the truth as I see it, sir. And you, I fear, are a coward."

From the corner of her eye she saw Drake shaking his head violently, but she ignored him. Hawkins appeared to be trying to decide whether or not he would strike her, and finally got the better of himself.

"It is time, ma'am, that you learned that someone aside from yourself is in control here," he said, his voice still thick with anger. "When I leave you here with the two you appear so concerned about, perhaps you will sing a different tune. I should imagine that when I come back later tonight, when it is cold and the rats have come out to play, that you will be kinder in manner to me."

Vivian lifted one shoulder pettishly, determined not to give him the satisfaction of a reply. He jerked her toward him, lifting her chin.

"I don't even feel any deep desire to kiss you," he said, pushing her to the floor. "It is too bad that you aren't a handsome wench."

"And, I am certain, Mr. Hawkins, that you can imagine how sorry I am that you don't find me pleasing," she replied dryly, rubbing her scraped elbow thoughtfully as she stared up at him.

He had lifted his hand to strike her, and Vivian could hear Drake trying to pull himself upright behind her, when a strong hand clamped down upon Hawkins's arm.

"I would not do that, Hawkins," remarked Lord Winter casually, quite as though he were suggesting that Hawkins not order a particular item from the bill of fare at some country inn. "Striking females is a bad business, you know. It will always come back to haunt you."

Hawkins cast him a glance of hatred, but he lowered his hand and moved away from Vivian.

"Allow me, Miss Reddington," said Lord Winter kindly, helping her to her feet and dusting her gown. "I am afraid that you were hardly used just now. My most sincere apologies. Hawkins is, as you so aptly hinted, a boor." And he swept her a graceful bow as he guided her to a keg for a makeshift chair.

Hawkins muttered angrily, but Winter ignored him, settling Vivian as comfortably as possible in the circumstances.

"Then why, sir, do you have any dealings with him?" she asked frankly, quite as though the subject of the conversation were not present, growling like a mastiff barely restrained by his chain.

His eyes lighted with appreciation at her forthright remark, but he shook his head regretfully. "I am sorry to admit it, but for the moment we are business partners, dear lady. It is quite unavoidable or I would not subject either of us to such an experience."

"That is a very poor excuse, sir," she replied, looking him straight in the eye.

"I knew you would find it so."

"Enought of that!" growled Hawkins. "Tie her up and have done with it, man! We have work to do!"

"Tie me up!" exclaimed Vivian. "Will you do so?"

"Indeed I will! And I'll be searching her for that snuff box, too!'' Hawkins reached for her, but Lord Winter neatly cut him off, elbowing him sharply into the wall.

"You will not touch her, Hawkins," he said coolly. "Do I make myself clear?"

Hawkins rubbed the side of his head and growled again.

"I am glad that we understand one another," Winter responded. "I must ask you, Miss Reddington," he continued, turning back to her, "if Hawkins is right and if you indeed have the silver snuff box that was once in Mr. Wilding's possession."

Vivian stared at him and shook her head. "No, I do not, sir," she replied, "but what if I did? What is that to you? Did it not belong to Mr. Wilding?"

Lord Winter shook his head. "I greatly fear that it is mine," he said apologetically, "although other people appear to feel that it is also theirs." He glanced at Hawkins, who glared at him malevolently. "It is a most inconvenient attitude."

"You may search me," she replied. "I do not have the box."

"Tempting though that suggestion is, Miss Reddington, I will not do so. You have never—" here he paused momentarily, as though in thought, and then corrected himself "—almost never given me any reason to doubt your word."

Flushing at this allusion to her book, Vivian dropped her eyes, then noticed that he was picking up the ropes that Hawkins had dropped.

Vivian watched him in disbelief. *"You* will bind me, sir?"

Winter nodded apologetically as he bound her wrists. "As much as I regret it, Miss Reddington, I fear it is a necessity— as much for your own safety as our own."

Vivian turned her face to the wall so that she would not be forced to look at him, but he finished knotting the cords about her wrists, then checked them to be certain they were not too tight.

"And I do regret it, my dear," he said in a low voice.

"Here now! Gag her and tie her ankles, too, man!" said Hawkins sharply.

"I think not," replied Lord Winter. "Where will she be able to go with her hands tied? She cannot open any door to leave here. And even if she screamed, who could hear her?"

Still grumbling, Hawkins left with him, abandoning the three left in the cellar to their own devices. Vivian looked about carefully, trying to determine if there were anything that she could use to her advantage. The candlestick had been left on the floor of the cellar, and its light wavered uncertainly in the darkness. Vivian settled herself beside it and carefully held her wrists, bound in front of her, over the flame. Bit by bit she burnt the cord away, scorching the tender flesh of her arms as well, but considering the result worth the pain. Finally the cords gave way and she hurried to Drake's side. In the pocket of her riding habit was his old knife, the one she always carried with her. She hadn't been able to use it for herself, but now she was able to rapidly free Drake and Ben, and to loosen their gags. Ben was still unconscious, but Drake was fully alert.

"What were you trying to do? Get yourself killed?" he whispered as soon as she had removed the gag. "Don't you know what Hawkins is like?"

She made a face. "Of course I do. I don't know what Lord Winter is doing with him, but I do know Hawkins's reputation. What I don't know is what you are doing here in beard and moustache."

Drake put his finger to his lips and pointed to Ben, who still appeared to be unconscious. "No one knows who I am," he whispered, "and I have to keep it that way."

Eager though she was to ask questions, Vivian held them back and gave her attention to Ben, loosening his collar while Drake chafed his wrists to restore circulation. Taking his pocket flask, she held his head in her lap and let a little of the brandy roll down his throat. He choked at first, but at last his eyes opened and appeared to focus on her.

"Are you all right, Ben?" she asked, worried by his silence.

"Did I not tell you, Miss, that you must give over coming here?" he said hoarsely. "This was a crackbrained thing for you to do."

She laughed. "I can see that you are feeling more yourself, Ben. We need to get you upstairs and care for that wound."

He shook his head. "Not upstairs, Miss. They'll be up there laying their plans. If they catch sight of us, we'll be back down here, tied up again—or worse."

"What plans, Ben?" Vivian demanded. "What are they planning to do?"

"Robbery, Miss," he said grimly. "They're no better than common thieves."

"Who are they going to rob?" she asked, puzzled.

"The three big houses in our parts—and Trevelyan is one of them."

Vivian stared at him, then her eyes flew to Drake. He nodded.

"So it would be our house, and Tom's, and Squire Trelawney's," she mused slowly. "And it will be tonight? All three of them?"

Again both men nodded. "They'll make a rich haul tonight," Drake said, "and when the delivery is made here at The Drawing Room, all of their booty will be taken safely away. This is just the beginning of Hawkins' plan for raiding along the coast."

"Are they looking for anything in particular?" asked Vivian, looking at Drake.

"Silver, jewelry, all portable property," replied Ben. "And it will all go into Boney's treasure chest."

"Bonaparte?" asked Vivian, startled. She had thought the men would be robbing for themselves, particularly Hawkins. "Hawkins is working for Bonaparte?"

Ben and Drake nodded. "They will be looking for the snuff box, too," said Drake, "the one that Hawkins mentioned to you, Miss. The one carried by a Mr. Wilding."

She nodded. "I know that box," she replied. "Mr. Wilding showed it to me. Why do they want it?"

"I suppose for its value," remarked Drake. "It is inset with jewels, many of them quite fine." He looked at her for a moment, considering the conversation about the snuff box that they had heard.

"What did they mean when they said that Roger Wilding no longer had the box? Was it stolen from him?"

Vivian shook her head. She hated to do what she was about to do, but she did not see that she had a choice. She could not confide in Drake as though she knew him well and not give them away to Ben.

"I don't believe so," she replied.

"How can they be so certain that he no longer has it?" he asked.

"Mr. Wilding had an accident at Lover's Leap," said Vivian slowly, avoiding her brother's eyes. "He was found at the bottom of the cliff."

There was a sudden, sharp silence, but Drake could not allow Ben—or anyone who happened to hear him—suspect that he had known Wilding or had connections in this part of the country. "How unfortunate!" said Drake in a hollow voice.

She nodded, trying to think of a way to soften the blow, to let him know that Wilding was indeed all right, but she could think of nothing.

As dusk fell that evening, the three of them slipped out into the cave where Pimm was secured, and quietly made their way out to the public road. Ben was going to make his way as quickly as possible to Squire Trelawney, not only to warn him of the robbery, but to notify him as magistrate that such an outrage was planned. Drake and Vivian were going to Trevelyan, hopeful that they would be able to convince John that it was necessary to do something to protect them.

"Will you actually go in, Drake?" she asked. "Will you let them see you even though it gives away your secret?"

He shrugged. "I suppose I'll have to, if we are to convince them that we must take steps to handle tonight's problem."

Vivian grinned. "I'd give a monkey to see Lacey's face when you walk in. I don't know who will be more taken aback—her or John."

"You give me so much to look forward to, Viv," he said lightly. "This would be a happy homecoming if it weren't for—" His voice grew gravelly and he stopped.

It dawned on Vivian that she had become so caught up in the thought of the robberies that she had not yet told him about finding Mr. Wilding intact, nor the whereabouts of the snuff box, but before she could say anything, they were at the doors of Trevelyan. It was dinnertime, and everyone had gathered in the drawing room. They could see them through the French windows as they neared the terrace.

There was a brief silence when they made their unexpected entrance. It took a moment or two for the others to recognize Drake behind his beard, but his mother was first to hurry forward and throw her arms about him.

"Drake! My dearest boy, whatever are you doing here?" she exclaimed, embracing him.

Lacey's eyes were wide. She was standing beside John, who scarcely looked delighted to see his brother home from the wars. "Drake," he said without enthusiasm, "what brings you to Trevelyan?"

Drake was not the only surprise guest, however. There was a sudden clearing of the throat at the other entrance to the drawing room and everyone turned.

"Drake! My dear fellow, I have so much to tell you! You won't believe the things that have befallen me."

Mrs. Reddington uttered a brief shriek as everyone stared. In the doorway stood Mr. Wilding.

Chapter Nineteen

Never did a corpse look as refreshed as did Mr. Wilding. Recovering from the singular reception given him by his hostess, he surged forward to greet her and the other members of the household, unaware that they regarded him as a Lazarus in their midst. Not until Vivian reminded him that he was supposed to have kept to his room did he recall their plan.

"Do you mean that he has been here at Trevelyan all this time that we thought he was dead?" demanded Mrs. Reddington. "Well, really, that was too bad of you both." She glared at Vivian and Tom. "How could you let us believe the poor man was dead when he was really upstairs dining on jam tart and beefsteak?"

"Not jam tart and beefsteak," remarked Mr. Wilding in a tone of distinct regret. "Cold lamb and a bit of kidney pie—and brandy, of course, for medicinal purposes."

"I am still awaiting an explanation," said Mrs. Reddington.

"And you shall have one, Mama," Drake assured her, "for

much of this can be laid at my door. But first we have an emergency to deal with.''

"An emergency?'' inquired John, his brows high. "What type of emergency, Drake? I trust that you are not going to be melodramatic.''

"I don't know, John, that I am going to be able to avoid it. You see, we are about to be robbed.''

Everyone, Mr. Wilding included, stared at him.

"Robbed?'' exclaimed Mrs. Reddington. "How do you know that, Drake? Thieves don't normally send out engraved announcements, so how do we know?''

"You will have to take my word for it, Mama. James Hawkins is planning to raid our home, and Tom's, and the Squire's.''

"Are you quite certain, Drake?'' asked John sharply.

He nodded. "A messenger has been sent to the Squire—and Tom's house is the farthest away of the three, so if we can stop them here, there should be no problem for those at his home.''

"Stop them?'' asked Lacey. "How can we possibly stop them?''

"By careful planning,'' Drake replied. "They won't be prepared for any sort of prepared resistance. They are expecting to take us by surprise.''

He put his hand on Tom's shoulder. "Tom, you go down to the stables and gather up the stablehands. Mama, you call in the footmen.''

"What would you like for me to do?'' asked John, unwilling to be left out.

"You think of a way to keep them from breaking down the front door or breaking open the terrace doors,'' Drake replied.

Mr. Wilding, who was still mulling over the matter of the engraved announcements, suddenly burst forth with, "Don't believe they usually do it at all, old fellow!''

"Who does what at all?" inquired Drake patiently.

"Send engraved announcements—the thieves, I mean, to their victims. A convenient idea, that, but I never heard of it being done."

John stared at him impatiently. "Don't be absurd, Wilding!" he snapped. "Keep your mind upon your business."

Mr. Wilding looked at him disapprovingly. "Don't have a business, Reddington. Seems to me that you would know I wouldn't. Not the thing at all for a gentleman, you know."

John gave it up and turned away, ready to give his attention to defending the entrance to the house.

Vivian turned to Drake apologetically. "I didn't mean to leave you in the dark about Mr. Wilding," she told him. "We just became so involved in other things that I didn't think of it."

He smiled. "That isn't a problem, Viv. It was worth it just to see him rise from the dead as he did tonight." His smile faded. "I do wish that he had managed to hang on to the snuff box, though."

She lowered her voice. "He did. I have it, Drake, in Papa's hiding place."

He threw his arm around her shoulders. "Good for you, Viv. I knew you would stay on top of things. After I took it from Hawkins, I had to get rid of it immediately. Now we only have to decipher the note in the box and we're home free."

"I've done that, too," she responded diffidently, afraid that she had taken too much upon herself.

Drake stared at her. "You already have it?" he asked in disbelief. "I worked for hours and didn't get anywhere."

Quietly she repeated the message and told him how she had deciphered it.

"Does the box belong to Lord Winter, Drake, and is the message his, also?" she asked.

He nodded. "He hasn't had it in his hands since he was

engaged to Lady Connaught years ago. She took it when she broke their engagement and ran away.''

Vivian stared at him in disbelief. ''She stole it? Why would she have done such a thing?''

Drake shrugged. ''She knew it was valuable itself, and she knew too that Winter prized it because it had belonged to his brother—although clearly he didn't know its importance.''

''What is Lady Connaught doing here?'' she asked. ''I saw her last night at The Drawing Room.''

''Hawkins,'' he responded briefly. ''They have been connected for years. And Winter, of course, both because he has money and is a part of the smuggling trade like her late husband and Hawkins, and because they can't be absolutely certain that I am the one who took the snuff box and gave it to Wilding.''

''What I would like to know, Drake,'' she said in a low voice, ''is how Lord Winter fits into all of this. I can't believe that he's really a part of something underhanded.''

He looked at her sympathetically. ''He's tied up with Hawkins, as you saw this afternoon. He has been for years. Hawkins works for Boney, and, from the look of things, Winter does, too. Is he a friend of yours, Viv?''

''My fiancé,'' she said, her tone bleak. ''Or at least he was,'' she corrected herself, ''until my book was published.''

Drake stared at her. ''You were engaged to Winter?'' he asked in disbelief. ''And you had a book published?''

He sat down. ''It appears that I have been out of touch for longer than I had realized.''

Mr. Wilding emerged from the brown study into which he had fallen. ''Did my best, Drake,'' he said solemnly. ''I give you my word. Did my best.''

Drake shook his hand gravely, having not the slightest idea which way the conversation was about to move. ''I know you did. And I am most grateful.''

Mr. Wilding nodded. ''Not an easy thing, I can tell you.

Knew you wouldn't like Winter as a brother-in-law. Stands to reason—the man's a spy for Boney. You're not. Bound not to like it.''

"Just so," Drake agreed. They mulled over the matter in silence for a few moments.

"Drake, how did Hawkins come to have you tied up with Ben? What were you doing at The Lighthouse?"

Drake grinned at her. "Remember all the hair-raising tales you used to read about the Terror and about brave Englishmen that risked their lives to save members of the French nobility just as they were being led away to the guillotine?"

She nodded.

"It seems that Winter's brother was just such a man—except that he was trying to help Marie Antoinette and Louie.''

Vivian's eyes grew wide. "You mean that he was trying to help them escape to England?"

"That's what the stories say. But he was killed before it could be brought to pass.''

She stared at him. "What does any of this have to do with Wellington and Napoleon today, Drake? What you're talking about is ancient history.''

He shook his head. "Not so ancient, it seems. The king and queen had been smuggling money and jewels out of the country so that they would have something to live upon when they finally made their escape. No one knows where it is—but we want to find it before Boney's people do so that it doesn't finance any of his campaigns.''

"And that's what you've been trying to find out?" she asked, trying to piece it all together.

"Not all of the smugglers are in the pay of the French," he said. "We have our own sources, and one of them had told us about Hawkins—although he called himself by another name then and worked a different coastline—and about the snuff box he had that he bragged had been a token of favor from the

French queen. Rumor had it that there was a message of some kind in the box as well.''

"That sounds like Hawkins," she agreed grimly, "taking credit for something that he had absolutely nothing to do with. And saying too much about it."

Drake nodded. "We already knew a little about him, but he suddenly disappeared the last time our people were getting too close to him. We didn't know where he was until I got your letter. No one considered the possibility that he might go to earth in such an out-of-the-way place as the Bristol Channel."

"So it was my letter that brought you here," she said, amazed by the idea—and a little saddened. It seemed that her writing—whether letters or books—had done nothing but bring down trouble upon Lord Winter. It had been an ill day for him when he encountered her.

Drake grinned at her. "I knew that you'd enjoy that. You always wanted adventure and here it is, my dear. There have been rumors at headquarters for months that Boney has been filling his treasury with English money, and that he has strong connections with smugglers all along the English coast. After you commented in your letter that there was more smuggling going on here and that a man, a newcomer, was trying to control it, headquarters thought that I would be the best person to look into the matter. Home turf, you know."

There was a sudden stirring as the stablehands, uncomfortable in their new surroundings, were brought into the house to protect the entrance, and the footmen gathered with them, arming themselves with rakes and cudgels and rolling pins. The rest of the servants, the women and the elderly butler, huddled together in the kitchen under the care of Mrs. Reddington and Lacey. Drake, taking a delegation of some of the largest men, began a tour of the house to post sentries at the locked doors and larger windows.

In the midst of the confusion, one of the stableboys pulled

at his forelock and handed Vivian a note. Unfolding it quickly, she read it, glanced round to see if anyone were watching, then put it away. Slipping quietly into the library, she closed the door, placed a chair in front of it, and carefully removed the snuff box from its hiding place, stowing it once more in her pocket.

In the midst of the bedlam in the hall, she caught Tom by the elbow before he could bustle away to give more orders to the frightened servants. "Where's Joe?" she asked, looking over the stablehands that had come in with him. Joe, she thought, could be of help to her now.

Tom thought for a moment, then shook his head. "I haven't seen him, Viv. Maybe he's on his way up now."

"I'll just slip down and see about Pimm and Joe," she said, moving toward the French windows. "I wouldn't want either of them to get hurt in all of this."

"Here now, Viv!" he shouted, outraged. "You can't be going off on your own like that! Come back here!"

His words were wasted, however. The window stood open and Vivian had slipped away into the darkness.

Mouthing imprecations and promising impossible acts of vengeance when he got his hands upon her, Tom set forth to find her, leaving John and Mr. Wilding in charge of marshaling the stablehands.

Discretion caused Tom to move quietly, aware that if he encountered anyone in the darkness—except for Vivian, of course—it could very likely be someone belonging to the Hawkins gang. Therefore, when he heard movement in the stable as he approached, he slipped into the shadows instead of moving straight into sight. As he inched his way around to where he could see into the stable, which was lighted by a single lantern, he heard a rustle behind him. He turned quickly, but not quite quickly enough. The blow fell just behind his ear, and Tom collapsed into a heap.

Vivian patted him gently on the head. "I'm sorry, Tom, but you can't come along this time."

Knowing that she was taking a terrible chance and fearing that she might meet the gang on its way to Trevelyan, Vivian hurriedly saddled Pimm and led him as quietly as possible away from the stable. There had been no sign of Joe, and Tom was still lying in the stableyard. She had confidence in his hard head, however, and was certain that he would revive in short order and again take his place in the house. In the meantime, she was going to The Drawing Room.

She fingered the paper in her pocket—and the snuff box. She was going to meet Lord Winter. It was more than time for them to have a talk.

The ride was blessedly uneventful, and she arrived all too soon at the rocky path that led down to the entrance to The Drawing Room. It looked even less inviting than she remembered it, but reminding herself that Winter was waiting—and that she had already treated him as shabbily as possible—she forced herself to begin her slow descent. She slipped only twice, catching herself each time before any damage could be done. No lights flashed back and forth between ship and shoreline tonight, no ship bobbed at anchor. All was quiet.

As she neared the mouth of the cave, her heart was beating rapidly—not from physical exertion, but from the thought of speaking with Lord Winter once more. Once more light gleamed from within the cave, a single bright lantern shedding its brilliance in the darkness.

"Lord Winter?" she called softly as she entered, thinking that he must be standing among the shadows.

She detected a movement, and a dark form wrapped in a cloak stepped forward, but it was not Lord Winter.

"How delightful to see you again, Miss Reddington," said Lady Connaught, her hood slipping back from her raven-wing hair.

"Lady Connaught!" she gasped. "What are you doing here?"

"Waiting for you, my dear," she replied sweetly. "I knew that if I put Winter's name to the note you would come immediately."

"Then he doesn't know that I'm here?" she asked, disappointment washing over her like a tidal wave.

"Oh, he knows," said Lady Connaught. "but I would scarcely allow him to see you alone. It wouldn't be wise. I already knew that he had an unreasonably strong fondness for you, and Hawkins told me what he did for you this afternoon. The fool! Falling for youth and—" here she looked Vivian up and down "—and undistinguished beauty when he could have had me! It is obvious that Richard is aging."

Vivian stared at her. "Why did you send the note, Lady Connaught?" she asked, puzzled. "Why should you wish to see me when you dislike me so?"

Lady Connaught laughed. "Because I want you to tell me, my dear, where the snuff box is. While the others are risking their lives and their freedom in those ill-advised robberies, I am going to seize the greatest prize for myself and leave. I have always fancied life in Rome—that box should supply me with enough to keep me for the rest of my days."

Vivian looked at her blankly, suddenly burningly aware of the silver box in her pocket. "I can't think what you mean, Lady Connaught. I've seen the box, of course—Mr. Wilding showed it to us just before his death—but I don't know where it is."

"I am quite certain that you know its whereabouts," Lady Connaught returned stubbornly. "You are not a beauty, but you are clever enough—I have watched you."

Vivian inclined her head in acknowledgement of the compliment. "You are very kind, ma'am, but I fear you overestimate my abilities. If I had the box, I would turn it over to you gladly, even though it isn't yours.''

''And whose do you think it is?'' demanded Lady Connaught. ''Richard's? He took that from the body of his dead brother, the brother he murdered! He told me so himself!''

Vivian frowned. ''You are lying, Lady Connaught. I don't believe that Lord Winter would have done such a thing. That is in your style, perhaps, and that of Mr. Hawkins—but not Lord Winter.''

''You besotted little fool!'' she snapped, jerking Vivian toward her. ''I suppose we'll have to do this the hard way after all.''

Vivian flinched as Lady Connaught caught hold of her wrist. Seeing this, the lady jerked off Vivian's riding gloves, exposing the bandages around her burns. ''So that is how you got loose,'' she commented, laughing. ''They thought it must have been one of the men who managed to free himself, but I was quite sure you were the one.''

''Why not let me go?'' asked Vivian, seizing upon this. ''I can be of no use to you, Lady Connaught.''

''Oh, but that is where you are so very wrong, my dear child,'' she replied, knotting a cord so firmly about Vivian's wrists that she winced in pain as it bit into the burned flesh. Picking up the lantern and pulling Vivian after her, Lady Connaught led her a little distance back into the cave.

''My dear Richard,'' she said gently, leaning over him with the lantern. ''Have you been listening?''

There was no reply, for he was both bound and gagged, but his eyes were bright and warm as he looked up at Vivian. Throwing her captive down and working quickly, Lady Connaught had soon tied Vivian's ankles together and gagged her, too.

''I'm afraid that there will be no candle left this time, Miss Reddington,'' she remarked cheerfully. ''Nor a lantern, either.

When all of this is over tonight and they bring their prizes back to be loaded upon the ship, we will pick you up as well. There will most certainly be casualties tonight, so it will come as no surprise when your bodies are found with the others.''

There was no reply, of course, as she stood smiling down at them. ''I would like to thank you, Richard, for your kindness in naming me your heir. It is a sad thing, of course, that your title dies with you, but at least I will make good use of your fortune—and of course I *am* already *Lady* Connaught, so it is not too much of a hardship.''

He did not give her the satisfaction of even the blink of an eye, so she turned to Vivian. ''And you, Miss Reddington— since you are so certain of Richard's innocence in the matter of his brother, it will surely be a comfort to you to die with him—and to know that we will undoubtedly find the snuff box and put its contents to good use.''

Lord Winter looked at Vivian, his dark eyes glowing, but Vivian's eyes were fixed upon Lady Connaught—for behind her moved several stealthy shadows.

''Here now! That will be enough of that, ma'am!'' said Tom abruptly, seizing Lady Connaught. Mr. Wilding caught up the lantern and held it high while Drake untied Vivian, and Ben Marley stood looking uncertainly down at Lord Winter.

''Should I loosen his bonds?'' he asked Drake.

''Yes, yes, of course you should, Ben!'' responded Vivian quickly.

Drake nodded, a little hesitantly however, and they stood looking down at him. Ignoring them, Vivian began unbinding him herself as soon as she was free.

''Are you so certain of my innocence, then, Miss Reddington?'' he asked, after she had removed the bandana tied round his mouth.

Vivian nodded. ''I have been certain this long time, sir.''

Pulling the snuff box from her pocket, she handed it to him. "This is yours, I believe."

There was an intake of breath from Lady Connaught and Drake. Lady Connaught began to laugh, almost hysterically. "So you had it with you all the time I was talking to you!" she exclaimed. "I didn't think of that for a moment, for I was certain that you had hidden it away, being much too clever to carry it about."

Lord Winter ran his fingers over the top of the box. "Thank you, Miss Reddington," he said gently. "My brother was carrying this when he was shot down and killed as we tried to escape some French ruffians who were pursuing us. I kept it as a remembrance of him until—until my unfortunate engagement to that lady, who stole it when she broke our engagement and ran away with Hawkins."

"But why didn't you decipher the note inside it?" asked Vivian, puzzled.

He shrugged. "I was only seventeen when I went with my brother on his last secret trip to France. When he was shot and died in my arms, I knew nothing of what he was doing—except that he was trying to help people escape. After his death I cared about nothing at all—certainly not about those who had been the cause of his death. The box was a memento of him, but the note inside it meant nothing. I left it there simply because he had placed it there."

"Then you don't know what it means?" she demanded.

He shook his head. "I knew that it had received some attention in recent days, of course, but I really knew nothing about it. Is it of any importance any longer?" he inquired.

"I should say that it is!" exclaimed Drake. "It seems that Marie Antoinette left money in the Bank of England in the name of Madame Papillon. You and your brother are named as her emissaries to that bank in the note. Wellington wishes to be certain that that money does not go to the coffers of Napoleon.''

Lady Connaught began to laugh again. ''And did the little one work out the note, too?'' she asked. ''What a merry chase she will lead you, Richard! I almost feel sorry for you.''

Suddenly Vivian remembered James Hawkins and the intended robberies and she seized Drake's arm. ''What has happened at home?'' she asked. ''Did they attack? Is everyone all right?''

Her brother patted her hand comfortingly. ''They never had the opportunity to do so. When Ben got to Squire Trelawney's, he wasn't the first one to lodge information against Hawkins and inform the squire that there would be robberies tonight. He had already sent a message to Lieutenant Waring, who gathered every able-bodied man available in the area of Grassmere to surround it. When Hawkins rode out, suspecting nothing, Waring arrested him.''

''Who went to the Squire?'' asked Vivian.

Drake nodded toward Lord Winter. ''This gentleman did so,'' he replied, ''and he told the Squire that he was willing to testify to it in a court of law.''

Vivian looked at him with wide eyes. ''What a very good story that would make!'' she exclaimed.

''Viv! Will you never learn your lesson!'' exclaimed Tom. ''If you hadn't written your frippery story about Winter the first time, Lacey would have had nothing to publish and you would have had no problem!''

Lord Winter glanced up sharply. ''Miss Lavenham published your book?'' he asked, looking at Vivian.

She nodded, her color rising. ''But Tom is right, of course. She couldn't have done so had I not written it originally. Although I did truly scratch out almost everything after I had met you and talked with you.''

Lord Winter laughed. ''I believe you, my dear—and I can't

tell you how that eases my mind. I had thought you had said all those things after—after we knew one another.''

She shook her head firmly. ''And I won't write any more stories about you, Lord Winter—I give you my word on that.''

There was a pause while she looked speculatively at Mr. Wilding. ''Although I would like to know, sir, why you kidnapped poor Mr. Wilding and set it about that he had gone head over heels over the cliff.''

Wilding nodded. ''Just so, Miss Reddington—very good question, very good, indeed. Explain yourself, sir!'' And he watched Lord Winter intently.

''Because the others suspected that you, sir—'' and here he nodded at Drake ''—had taken the snuff box from Hawkins, having spent some time with him coming over from France to pick up a shipment and having shown a great interest in it. They were watching you, and so knew that Mr. Wilding had called upon you at a rather late hour, and that he had ridden down from London particularly to do so. When they kidnapped you and did not find it, they knew that taking it from Mr. Wilding would be an easy matter. And accidents happen readily on the cliffs. I simply moved more quickly than did they.''

Mr. Wilding seized his hand and pumped it up and down. ''And I thank you for it, sir, I thank you! It was damnably uncomfortable in that inn, but better, sir, far better than resting at the bottom of the cliffs.''

Lord Winter managed to disengage himself. ''I am relieved that you feel that way, sir. But I will say,'' he said, turning to Vivian and Tom, ''that you two are the very devil for getting in the way. No sooner did I get Mr. Wilding safely put away than the two of you came along, poking and prying and asking questions and calling unnecessary attention to yourselves.''

Tom started to protest, but thought better of it, and Vivian took Lord Winter's arm as he led her from The Drawing Room to the shadowy beach in front of it. A bright moon was rising, its light shining on the box in Winter's hand. He slipped it into his pocket and pulled her close to him.

"You are far too much trouble when you are out of my sight, Miss Reddington. If I promise that you will have time for your writing and that I will never press you to attend a ball, will you consider marrying me?"

Epilogue

And so it was that a year later Vivian was looking proudly down at a copy of her newest novel, *The Last Love.*

Lord Winter was staring at it dubiously. "Will it be safe for our friends to read this?" he inquired.

"Don't be so nervous, Richard," she reassured him. "You are in it only a very little bit."

"And what about the rest of us?" inquired Tom doubtfully, balancing his godson carefully in his arms. "Are any of us in your story this time, Viv?"

She paused for a moment, then smiled wickedly. "I shall let you find that out for yourself, Tom—which means that you will have to read the book, a thing you haven't done since Mr. Crewett forced you to do so."

Tom colored. "I'm not as bad as all that, Viv. I do read now and then—the paper and whatnot." Reference to the paper reminded him of his news and his face brightened. "I saw the announcement of John's wedding." He grinned. "I have seldom heard of a more suitable match," he added, handing the baby to Mr. Wilding, who blanched and shrank back, pleading the crispness of his cravat as excuse.

"Nonsense, Wilding! You have to become accustomed to our godson," Tom told him firmly, placing the infant carefully in his victim's arms.

"But I can become accustomed to him from over here," protested Mr. Wilding, moving to a place of safety behind Mrs. Reddington. "I will take charge of him when it is time for him to learn to tie his cravat properly—certainly you could not teach him to do so."

Unperturbed by this assault upon his sartorial style, Tom bore down upon him, holding the baby before him like a weapon. Before he could make the final assault, however, Mrs. Reddington interfered, removing young Richard from potential disaster.

"I'll take my grandson, thank you, sir," she said crisply. "What he will do with three godfathers is more than I can understand, Vivian."

"Drake and Tom and Roger will take care of him very nicely, Mama," she replied. "Drake will make him a thinker and a military man, Roger will teach him to dress properly, and Tom will teach him how to be a nuisance."

She ducked as Tom sent a sofa cushion whizzing toward her. "Besides, they relieved me from the necessity of naming a godmother," she added. "Lacey would have expected me to ask her and I could not have brought myself to do it."

She chuckled. "I would love to see John's face when he discovers that Lacey plans to rule the roost—and to take charge of his finances. She doesn't approve of long trips to Scotland, either. She plans for him to sell that property and give up his fishing. If he weren't so completely self-absorbed, I would almost feel sorry for him."

"It will serve the old fellow right," grinned Tom. "If he

had paid attention to what we told him about her, he wouldn't have found himself living under the cat's paw.''

''I find that I can sympathize with my unfortunate brother-in-law,'' said Lord Winter gravely, looking down at Vivian.

''To be sure you can,'' agreed Tom, laughing as Vivian made a face at him.

He glanced at the cover of her book and smiled at her. ''And even though Lady Connaught was right, my dear, and you have led me a merry chase, I would do it all again.''

Lifting her hand to his lips, he added, ''You are my last—and my dearest—love.''

ABOUT THE AUTHOR

Mona Gedney lives with her family in West LaFayette, Indiana. She is the author of seven Zebra Regency romances and is currently working on a short story to be included in Zebra's June Bride Regency anthology, A BRIDE'S BOUQUET, to be published in May 1997. Mona loves hearing from her readers and you may write to her c/o Zebra Books. Please include a self-addressed stamped envelope if you wish a response.

WATCH FOR THESE ZEBRA REGENCIES

LADY STEPHANIE (0-8217-5341-X, $4.50)
by Jeanne Savery

Lady Stephanie Morris has only one true love: the family estate she has managed ever since her mother died. But then Lord Anthony Rider arrives on her estate, claiming he has plans for both the land and the woman. Stephanie soon realizes she's fallen in love with a man whose sensual caresses will plunge her into a world of peril and intrigue . . . a man as dangerous as he is irresistible.

BRIGHTON BEAUTY (0-8217-5340-1, $4.50)
by Marilyn Clay

Chelsea Grant, pretty and poor, naively takes school friend Alayna Marchmont's place and spends a month in the country. The devastating man had sailed from Honduras to claim his promised bride, Miss Marchmont. An affair of the heart may lead to disaster . . . unless a resourceful Brighton beauty finds a way to stop a masquerade and keep a lord's love.

LORD DIABLO'S DEMISE (0-8217-5338-X, $4.50)
by Meg-Lynn Roberts

The sinfully handsome Lord Harry Glendower was a gambler and the black sheep of his family. About to be forced into a marriage of convenience, the devilish fellow engineered his own demise, never having dreamed that faking his death would lead him to the heavenly refuge of spirited heiress Gwyn Morgan, the daughter of a physician.

A PERILOUS ATTRACTION (0-8217-5339-8, $4.50)
by Dawn Aldridge Poore

Alissa Morgan is stunned when a frantic passenger thrusts her baby into Alissa's arms and flees, having heard rumors that a notorious highwayman posed a threat to their coach. Handsome stranger Hugh Sebastian secretly possesses the treasured necklace the highwayman seeks and volunteers to pose as Alissa's husband to save her reputation. With a lost baby and missing necklace in their care, the couple embarks on a journey into peril—and passion.

Available wherever paperbacks are sold, or order direct from the Publisher. Send cover price plus 50¢ per copy for mailing and handling to Penguin USA, P.O. Box 999, c/o Dept. 17109, Bergenfield, NJ 07621. Residents of New York and Tennessee must include sales tax. DO NOT SEND CASH.